THE SURPRISE IN THE COFFIN

Morton groped his way down the stairs and found himself in a large chamber, half underground. In the flickering light, he could see that the walls were stacked with coffins. "That's the one," the chaplain pointed to a gleaming ebony coffin on the other side.

Morton, the sergeant and the two constables took hold of the coffin, slid it from its niche and stood back reverently. "Right!" cried Dr. Burney zestfully. "Now, sergeant, can we open him up? Screwdriver, screwdriver! Surely you've brought one."

Prior, young and white-faced, lunged down the steps, dropped the screwdriver in the sergeant's hands, and fled. "Here you are, Smith, you used to be a joiner, get the lid off." Smith began painstakingly to remove the long brass screws. Finally he stood back with a sigh of relief. "That's the lot."

"Well, what are you afraid of?" exclaimed the sergeant, and seized the top end of the lid and raised it. At that moment there was a crash of thunder from above, a gasp of horror from the sergeant, and a clatter as the coffin lid dropped to the floor.

DEATH
— OF AN —
HONOURABLE MEMBER

A Sergeant Bragg – Constable Morton Mystery

RAY HARRISON

BERKLEY BOOKS, NEW YORK

This Berkley book contains the complete
text of the original hardcover edition.
It has been completely reset in a typeface
designed for easy reading and was printed
from new film.

DEATH OF AN HONOURABLE MEMBER

A Berkley Book/published by arrangement with
Charles Scribner's Sons

PRINTING HISTORY
Scribner's edition published 1985
Berkley edition/November 1988

ISBN: 0-425-11189-X

A BERKLEY BOOK ® TM 757,375
Berkley Books are published by The Berkley Publishing Group
200 Madison Avenue, New York, NY 10016.
The name "Berkley" and the "B" logo
are trademarks belonging to Berkley Publishing Corporation.

PRINTED IN THE UNITED STATES OF AMERICA

10 9 8 7 6 5 4 3 2 1

To Nigel and Caron

CHAPTER ———— ———— ONE

Detective Sergeant Joseph Bragg of the City of London Police strode along Cheapside towards his office. He was conscious of being out of tune with his surroundings. The cloud and rain that made June miserable had hung on till the middle of July, but today the sun was shining from a placid blue sky, and everyone was smiling. A street orderly darted into the traffic and scooped up some horse droppings with a flourish; then, pirouetting like a matador between the lumbering vehicles, gained the pavement again.

Perhaps it was because the case at the Old Bailey had gone on well into the lunch hour; or maybe it was the stricken look on the face of the accused's wife when the guilty verdict had been given. So far as he could remember he'd felt content enough that morning. One thing was for sure: he'd never go to the Saracen again. The pint of beer he'd been served was flat and stale; and they'd charged him

1

tuppence for it. And their sausages had more bread than pork in them. Funny how the newspaper reporters managed to take over the Magpie and Stump. If you weren't there by one o'clock you could never get near the bar. God knows where they got their money from.

But at least the girls had forsaken their coats. A chattering group of them came towards him, wearing high-necked white blouses and long black skirts. Some of them were even without their hats. Probably typewriters from the Gresham Assurance. They glanced provocatively at him as he was forced to step into the gutter to let them pass, then burst into giggles as they scampered up the steps and through a doorway. Pretty, young and shapely: in ten years they'd look work-worn and defeated. But that was how they wanted it. A few years' fun, then marriage, children and penny-pinching. That was what life entitled them to, and they'd no more expect to change it than to become Queen of England.

As he turned into Old Jewry, its cool gloom seemed to confirm his jaundiced mood. He pulled out his watch. Nearly three o'clock. He'd never get his paperwork done by six. He hurried into the courtyard of the old Georgian mansion that served as the headquarters of the City Police, and made for the stairs.

'Joe!' called the desk sergeant. 'The Commissioner says he wants to see you the moment you get in.'

'Blast!' muttered Bragg. 'What for?'

'I dunno, but he didn't sound too pleased you weren't here. I wouldn't keep him waiting if I were you.'

Bragg walked through the empty ante-room and, rapping on the door, entered the Commissioner's office. Sir William Sumner was seated behind his desk staring irritably through the window, while a man Bragg didn't recognize sat dejectedly in front of it.

'Ah, there you are!' Sir William swung round as Bragg entered. 'I wondered where the devil you'd got to.'

When angry, the Commissioner's carefully cultivated resemblance to the Prince of Wales went awry, and he became a spluttering army officer again, thinking he was God.

'You know Dr Primrose, the coroner, I take it?'

The man by the desk raised his head, and nodded briefly at Bragg. It seemed hardly possible that it could be so. Granted the coroner was small and bird-like, but this man looked shrunken. Whatever had passed between them before Bragg's arrival had not been pleasantries. From the tension in the room he guessed they had sat unspeaking for some time, waiting for him to come.

'I suppose you might as well sit down, Bragg,' said Sir William ungraciously. 'Dr Primrose wants to explain something to you.'

Bragg carried a bentwood chair from the window and placed it opposite the coroner. Now he could see that his face was grey and strained, and his eyes red-rimmed from lack of sleep.

The coroner cleared his throat and looked around him, almost in parody of his courtroom mannerisms. 'Sergeant Bragg,' he began, 'Sir William has agreed to do me a considerable favour, and has placed your services at my disposal. Rather, I should say, made them available to carry out certain enquiries, since in the circumstances it would be improper for me to direct them myself.'

The coroner looked for help, or comfort, towards the Commissioner, but Sir William was grimly staring at the church tower across the road. Dr Primrose shifted his gaze to the desk, and, picking up a gilt-edged correspondence card from the blotter, handed it to Bragg. 'I received that by the first post yesterday morning.'

The writing was a meticulous copper-plate, spaced to elegantly fill the card. 'Our Honourable Member. Was it really an accident?' it read.

'What does it mean, sir?' asked Bragg.

The coroner took a deep breath, then let it go in a despondent sigh. 'I'm afraid it can only refer to the recent death of Sir Walter Greville, who as you know was one of the two Members of Parliament for the City of London. I have to tell you that I am conscious of a grave dereliction of duty in that regard, and if the verdict of my court proves to be unwarranted, I shall have no honourable alternative open to me, but to resign my office. I have therefore asked Sir William to nominate an experienced and discreet detective officer to determine if there is any substance to the innuendo on the card.'

The Commissioner swivelled back to his desk and took up a paper-knife, as if to defend himself from any involvement.

'I must give you a full account of what I know of the case,' the coroner went on. 'At the very least it may serve to relieve my own anxieties. Thereafter I shall take no part in overseeing your investigations. Sir William will keep me informed of their outcome.'

Bragg glanced at the Commissioner, but he was preoccupied with flexing the blade of his paper-knife.

'It was on the night of Friday the tenth of July that the death of Sir Walter took place. My wife and I had just returned from a dinner of the Worshipful Company of Skinners, at Dowgate Hill, and were preparing for bed, when there was a knock at the door. It proved to be the beadle for the Coleman Street ward. He asked me to go immediately to a house in Finsbury Circus, where there had been an accident. I replied that, as he well knew, I had not practised medicine for many years, and told him to go elsewhere. He said that the man concerned was Sir Walter Greville, and he was dead.

'I see now that I ought to have followed the normal procedures and instructed the police. I was conscious, however, of Sir Walter's position in society, and of the desirability of avoiding any untoward or scandalous publicity. And since I am the official charged with investigating unexpected death, I felt it was entirely proper that I should in this case discharge that function personally. I therefore acceded to the request, and went with the beadle. When we arrived the family physician was still there. He is Dr Graham who practises from Bell Yard nearby. You will be able to get a statement from him.' The coroner dropped his eyes to his hands, conscious that he had overstepped his self-imposed restrictions.

'Lady Greville was there also, and as you can imagine she was very distraught. She had come in shortly before and found her husband's body at the bottom of the stairs. It must have been a terrible shock. I was shown the body, which still lay where it had fallen. There was a severe wound in the head, but very little blood. The body was still warm, so death was comparatively recent. Dr Graham took me to the top of the stairs and showed me a loose stair rod. The carpet had wrinkled as a result, and it was evident that anyone might trip over the obstruction and be flung headlong down the stairs. Because of the position of the lights, that area of the staircase was in shadow. Dr Graham pointed out the carved newel post at the bottom of the stairs, and suggested that Sir Walter had tripped on the loose carpet, fallen down the stairs, and struck his head on the newel post. I returned to the body, and examined the wound on his head.'

The recollection seemed oddly unpleasant, thought Bragg, for a man who spent his official life sifting through the evidence of unnatural and violent deaths.

'I remarked that the normal procedures would demand a post-mortem examination, but, in view of the circumstances and the evidence as to the cause of death, I would dispense with it. I think Lady Greville was grateful for that. I authorized the body to be moved, and the doctor left, saying he would call on the undertaker. I felt it advisable to take Lady Greville home with me for the night.'

'Did you know the Grevilles, sir?' asked Bragg.

The coroner gave a resigned smile. 'Yes, we knew them, sergeant. It would be difficult to be an official in the City and not know the Grevilles . . . as Sir William can tell you.'

'And when was the inquest, sir?'

Primrose's eyes fastened on the brass drawer-handle by his chair. 'On Monday. I'm sure that the Press would regard it as perfunctory in the extreme. It was held in due form, naturally, and returned a verdict of accidental death. But I have to admit that few witnesses were called. Dr Graham gave evidence of identification, and the medical evidence on the cause of death. Lady Greville gave a brief account of finding her husband's body, and of the loose stair rod. I then directed the jury on the basis that the evidence pointed to accidental death, and they so found.'

'But now you're not so sure?' asked Bragg.

'Yes, yes, I am sure,' said the coroner sharply. 'There wasn't a shred of evidence to the contrary . . . But now this.'

'I suppose Sir Walter has been buried.'

'The funeral was yesterday.'

'The same day as you got this card.'

'Yes.'

'You didn't think to hold up the funeral, then?'

'It would not have been possible. It was taking place in

Hertfordshire at the family seat. In any case I took the view that the card was an unwarranted aspersion on the processes of my court.'

'And what has happened to change your mind?' asked Bragg.

'Nothing. I still believe it was accidental death. I am aware, however, that I am open to criticism for dispensing with a post-mortem examination. If the anonymous correspondent is prepared to direct this innuendo to me, he is liable to communicate the same calumny to the Press.'

'And what do you want of me?'

The coroner cleared his throat hesitantly. 'I would like you to make discreet enquiries to establish whether there is any reason to suppose that Sir Walter's death was other than by accident. In no way do I wish it to be handled as a normal police enquiry. That could prejudice the standing of the judiciary.'

Out of the corner of his eye Bragg saw Sir William's lip curl in scorn.

'But how will such enquiries prevent the writer of the card from communicating with the newspapers?' asked Bragg.

'I am assuming that he is someone close to the family. I feel that he will become aware of them and be satisfied.'

There was a momentary silence, and Bragg felt that the coroner's account had to some extent dissipated the tension.

'One more thing, sir.'

'Yes?' The coroner raised his eyes to Bragg's.

'If my enquiries suggest that Sir Walter's death was not accidental . . . ?'

'If you establish a *prima facie* case of unlawful killing, then the court's verdict will be set aside.' Primrose got to his feet. 'That is all I can tell you. Sir William, you know where to find me if I can be of further help.' He took his hat from the side table, nodded once more to Bragg, and was gone.

The Commissioner put down the paper-knife and looked truculently at Bragg. 'I want this job done quickly and quietly. Understand?'

'Yes, sir.'

'Drop everything you are doing, and concentrate on this alone. I want the answer in a fortnight.'

'Do I report to Inspector Cotton, sir?'

'No. You're on detached duty, with full discretion to pursue what enquiries you feel necessary. Report to me direct."

'It would be helpful if I could use Constable Morton as well,' remarked Bragg.

'Why?'

'If I can only investigate in an oblique way, it will take more time. Besides, his upper-crust background will make it easier for him to quiz these kind of people.'

'Very well. Let Inspector Cotton know. That will be all, Bragg.'

'Detached duty!' cried Inspector Cotton incredulously. 'Christ Almighty! I've little enough staff, without losing you two. What the hell's it all about?'

'I'm afraid I can't tell you, sir,' replied Bragg cautiously.

'Why not?'

'The Commissioner expressly instructed me to make these enquiries discreetly, and report only to him.'

'That doesn't bloody mean I'm not to know about it,' retorted Cotton angrily.

'I'm sure that's the case,' agreed Bragg, 'but I'd rather the Commissioner told you himself.'

'If you're working a flanker, Bragg, I'll have you on the beat again before you can break wind.'

'Yes, sir.'

'What about your other cases?'

'I was told to drop everything.'

'Drop . . . I'm not having this!' Cotton bounced out of his chair. 'We'll see what Forbes has to say about it.'

'I don't suppose the Chief Inspector knows yet, sir.'

'Well, I know one thing, Bragg. He won't stomach your going behind his back like this. You'd better watch your step, Commissioner or not!'

'Someone's written to the coroner about his honourable member.' Bragg flicked the spent match towards the empty grate. 'And we've got to look into it.'

'Sounds more like a job for Bart's Hospital than us,' remarked Morton with a grin.

'Our esteemed coroner has really kicked over the jerry this time. He cooked the inquest on Sir Walter Greville, to make sure the verdict was accidental death. Didn't bother with a post-mortem in case it raised inconvenient questions. Now some joker has sent him a card saying "Was it really an accident?" Got old Primrose in a fine sweat. Borrowed us from Sir William to mop up the mess.'

'I should think the Commissioner at least will enjoy this, after all the criticism we've had from the coroner recently.'

'You wouldn't think so. When I went in you'd have thought they'd just fought ten rounds . . . bare fisted. Sir William hardly spoke while the coroner was with us. I've never seen him so angry.'

'I'd have thought he would relish the chance of getting back at Primrose,' remarked Morton.

'Not a bit of it lad. These officials are all politicians at
bottom. Primrose knows that if this story got into the
papers, he would be finished. So he's involving the police
now, to try and prove the verdict was right all the time. He
as good as told me he only wanted to hear that Sir Walter's
death was an accident.'

'And is the Commissioner prepared to be used in this
way?'

'He's in a difficult position. Old Primrose is well-
connected in the City, with powerful friends on the
Common Council. He couldn't have baited the police over
the years otherwise. If Sir William had refused to help, it
would have seemed that he wanted Primrose discredited.
Equally, if we did an overt investigation and found it was
indeed an accident, it would look as if the Commissioner
was merely trying to smear the coroner.'

'And I suppose,' said Morton thoughtfully, 'that if we
make superficial enquiries which vindicate the coroner, and
it afterwards turns out that there was foul play, we could be
accused of covering up the truth to help him.'

'You're beginning to get the idea,' nodded Bragg,
tapping out his pipe on the massive glass ash-tray. 'And you
and I are really in the crap. According to the coroner, the
writer of the card is close to the family, hence his
suspicions. Primrose hopes that he will hear we are quietly
making enquires, and, when the case isn't reopened, will be
satisfied his fears were groundless. On that basis, if it isn't
obvious we are investigating, the writer will go to the
newspapers. But if we make it obvious, there are going to
be rumours, and the papers will get hold of it anyway.'

'So the Commissioner put us on detached duty, and gave
you full discretion, because we shall carry the can whatever
happens.'

'And all because the coroner was too pissed to think straight. Well, I'm no politician,' said Bragg, pushing back his chair. 'I'm just a stupid bloody copper, and my job's to find out the truth, whether it's to the liking of Sir William and Dr Primrose, or whether it's not.'

CHAPTER ———— ———— TWO

The Grevilles' house was in the north-west quadrant of Finsbury Circus. In other parts of the Circus, houses had been converted into offices. Their windows were uncurtained, their front doors ajar. Here not one brass plate demeaned the splendid Georgian sweep of the terrace. The windows were heavily draped, the steps spotless. Only the rich could afford to live here, and they exulted in their prosperity.

Number nine had been created by joining together two houses, giving a frontage of some sixty feet on five storeys. The curtains were half-drawn, and a large bow of black crepe hung from the door knocker. The house itself seemed detached from the demonstrations of grief within it. As if it were a manifestation of the City's commercial preeminence, which would last for centuries to come.

Bragg and Morton mounted the steps and rang the bell.

They waited for some time, then rang again. Just as they were about to turn away, they heard firm steps crossing the hallway. The door was opened by a middle-aged woman with greying hair, in a severe black dress.

'Lady Greville?' asked Bragg.

'I'm the housekeeper,' she replied sharply. 'Do you wish to see her ladyship?'

'Yes, please, madam,' replied Bragg. She eyed them dubiously. 'Who shall I say?' she asked.

'Sergeant Bragg and Constable Morton of the City Police.'

'You'd better come in.' She motioned them into the hallway and closed the door. 'I'll see if her ladyship can receive you.'

Bragg and Morton found themselves in a huge marble-floored hall that took up most of the ground floor. The contrast with the outside of the house was startling, for it had been remodelled as a gothic baronial hall. A refectory table occupied the middle of the room, between two stone pillars which took the place of the wall that must have been demolished. Beyond it was a huge fireplace, modelled, Morton suspected, on one he'd seen in the chateau at Blois. There were tapestries on the rough-plastered walls and Persian rugs on the floor, but the room was created for effect, not to live in. There were only two chairs, one on each side of the fireplace; their backs and arms so heavily carved they must have been painful to sit in. Stained glass panels had been installed inside the original sash windows, creating such an ecclesiastical gloom that even on this brilliant morning the sun could scarcely colour the grey marble.

'God Almighty!' muttered Bragg. 'What a place!'

'Strawberry Hill come to town,' suggested Morton.

'What? . . . I suppose that must be the staircase he fell down.'

At first sight it was impressive. It ran from a small landing just below ceiling height, straight along the wall to the floor of the hall itself. The steps were wide, the balusters of heavily carved oak, ending in a magnificent square newel post with grinning gargoyles projecting from each face. Parallel to the hand rail a row of eight niches had been contrived in the wall, each holding a small bronze statue. Following them upwards Morton realized that the staircase had been inserted under a comparatively small well at the back corner of the building. He could see the bottom of a door in the wall on the next storey, with two shallow steps leading to it from the landing. It was here that the scale of the would-be mediaeval hall clashed with the Georgian domestic architecture on which it had been imposed. A more critical examination of the steps showed them to be a steeper angle than normal. The staircase almost plunged to the floor of the hall, terminating opposite the front door and about fifteen feet from it.

'It's well enough lit at the moment,' remarked Bragg, 'with the window at the back in the stair-well. But at night it might not be, with just the gas brackets at top and bottom.'

'I'm surprised they haven't installed electric lighting,' replied Morton, 'though I suppose it would destroy the illusion.'

The door at the top of the stairs opened, and the hem of a black skirt appeared, held carefully away from a pair of elegant black shoes. The figure turned towards them, and had descended two stairs before they could see that it was a young woman of around thirty. Her pale face was heart-shaped, her eyes dark brown, and her hair dressed fashionably close to the head. With the plain skirt she wore a pearl-grey blouse, and a square of black crepe was thrown

over her shoulders. She advanced towards them from the
foot of the stairs, her arm across her breast.

'I'm sorry,' she said defensively, looking down at her
blouse. 'I hadn't expected anyone. I was just writing some
letters. I haven't got all my mourning clothes yet."

'Don't worry about us, your ladyship,' said Bragg
soothingly. 'We aren't exactly society people.'

She smiled mechanically. 'Why have you come to see
me?'

'The coroner pointed out that we hadn't got any papers
relating to your husband's death, so we're quickly putting a
file together.'

'I see. Very well. What do you want from me?'

'You found your husband's body it seems. What time was
that?'

'I can't be precise. It was such a shock, it all seems a
blur. I'd spent the evening with my old governess in the
mews cottage. It must have been eleven o'clock when I left
her. I came in through the front door . . . and there he
was.' Her voice faltered, and she turned her face away.

'What did you do then?' asked Bragg gently.

'I ran round the mews, and sent Tom, the coachman, for
Dr Graham. Then I came back here, to Walter.'

'Did you attempt to revive him?'

'No. I was frightened . . . he was so still. I just stayed
with him.'

'What happened then?'

'The doctor came. He turned Walter over. There was a
most terrible . . .' She flinched at the memory.

'Don't worry about that. The doctor can tell us.'

'Then John Primrose came,' she resumed, 'and took me
home with him.'

'What time would that have been?'

'About midnight.'

'And when did you come back here?'

'Late the next morning. Walter had been taken away . . .'

'Who made the arrangements for the funeral?'

'He has a cousin in Hertfordshire, where the funeral was held.'

'I see. Do you feel up to telling us how Sir Walter's body was lying?'

She dabbed her eyes with a black handkerchief. 'He was lying on his left side, so I couldn't see the . . .'

'The wound,' murmured Bragg. 'Where was he in relation to the staircase?'

'A short distance from the bottom of the stairs with his head towards the middle of the room.'

'Down you go, lad,' ordered Bragg. 'Now, your ladyship, let's try to get Constable Morton into the same position.'

'More across the bottom of the stairs, sergeant.'

Morton slid over a little.

'Were his legs straight out, or curled up?'

'One was straight out, the other bent . . . like this.'

She stooped and hesitantly pulled Morton's upper leg over.

'And his arms?'

'His right arm was in front of his face. I couldn't see the other.'

Morton pushed his left arm behind him.

'Is that better?' asked Bragg.

'I think so,' she hesitated. 'It's difficult because your constable is so much bigger than my husband.'

'Let's concentrate on the position of the head.'

'It was further back, nearer the stairs.'

'By the newel post?'

'Is that what you call it? . . . Yes.'

Morton wriggled across, and felt his foot touch the wall. Bragg pondered for a moment, gently pulling the corner of his ragged moustache. 'Right, lad,' he called. Morton stood up, and, as he brushed the dust from his clothes, saw a momentary look of vexation cross Lady Greville's face.

'Was your husband a heavy drinker?' asked Bragg.

'No. If anything he was an abstemious man. I've seldom seen him under the influence of drink.'

'Did he go out on Friday night, that you know of?'

'I don't think so. He had a political meeting here in the early evening. I left the house at half past six, and I think it was due to begin at seven.'

'What did he do about food?'

'The housekeeper provided a buffet supper for them, as usual.'

'Do you know who was at the meeting that night?'

'I know Hubert Winterslow was there. He'll be able to tell you.'

'Where does he live?'

'Somewhere in Coopers Row; by Trinity House.'

'We'll find him. Now, if you could show us the stair rod that was loose, you can leave us to finish on our own.'

'That's considerate of you, sergeant.' She turned towards the stairs.

'What a marvellous collection of bronzes,' remarked Morton conversationally. 'All mediaeval knights, but each slightly different, even to the coat-of-arms on the shield . . . Ah, there's a bronze of a woman in the middle; looks like a queen.'

'My husband was something of an aesthete.' She smiled sadly. 'He used to say it was me, as Guinevere, surrounded by Arthur and his knights.'

Morton picked up the statuette. 'Just look at the detail! It's beautiful.'

Lady Greville pointed to the second step from the top. 'That's the one.'

Bragg looked back down the staircase. 'And which end was loose?'

'The one by the wall.'

'Thank you, your ladyship. We won't be many minutes now.'

'You can let yourselves out.' She moved slowly up to the landing, and disappeared through the doorway.

'The coroner said the body was warm when he saw it at, say, half past eleven. Was last Friday a warm night, do you remember?' asked Bragg.

'Fairly. It was the first of the really sunny days.'

'Still, it would be pretty cool on the marble there . . . He could have walked down in the dusk, and tripped. Damn! We should have asked her whether the lights were on.'

'The coroner was right about the shadow, though. The wall-bracket on the landing is too low to illuminate the steps properly.'

'Just go up to that doorway will you, lad? And walk down the stairs at a normal speed.' Bragg took up a position on the landing.

Morton flattened his back against the door, then began walking casually down the stairs. Turning at the landing he kept to the wall, where the loose stair rod had been. As his foot touched the second step he felt a violent push between the shoulder-blades. He pitched forwards, hand scrabbling at the balusters, his feet tobogganing down the edges of the steps. He managed to grasp the stair-rail just as his left shoulder collided with one of the gargoyles.

'Well done, lad,' called Bragg cheerfully. 'Showed a treat how it could have happened.'

'My God!' complained Morton, rubbing his bruised

shoulder. 'I'll ask for a transfer back to the beat! What did you do that for?'

Bragg opened the door and went out into the street.

'Sorry, lad, but it was the only way to sort it out. You see, Lady Greville said his head was close by the newel post, and that didn't sound right.'

'Why's that?' asked Morton, falling into step beside him.

'We know Sir Walter was shorter than you are. So if he hit his head on one of those carvings he must have been fairly well upright.'

'Yes.'

'But if his feet had been close to the newel post at that point, he would have fallen away from it. You recollect she said one of his legs was straight, so it doesn't sound as if he crumpled up on the spot.'

'So what has your bit of mayhem proved?' asked Morton ruefully.

'I expected you to go down the stairs head first, you see.'

'She's right. You are considerate.'

'And your head wouldn't have been anywhere near the newel post. As it was you managed to keep upright by grabbing at the banisters, but the momentum took you right to the bottom.'

'Does that mean you are prepared to say it was an accident?' asked Morton.

''It could have been. We must find out what size shoes he took. After all, it might not work if he didn't have your great plates of meat!'

They ran Hubert Winterslow to earth in the echoing cavern of Billingsgate fish market, where he had a wholesaling business. He was a brisk, portly man of around fifty, with a balding head and luxuriant side whiskers.

'Come into the office,' he said genially. "There's not much doing at this time of day.'

They picked their way between piles of empty fish baskets into a tiny office at the back of the stall. Most of the available space was taken up by a desk covered with piles of papers. Morton elected to stand by the door, and Bragg squeezed into the uncomfortable-looking chair opposite the desk.

'I thought they'd brought it off as accidental death,' remarked Winterslow.

'That's true,' replied Bragg. 'We're just completing our papers.'

'Right then. Fire away.' Winterslow leaned back in his chair contentedly, and clasped his hands on his belly.

'I'm told that you were at a political meeting in Sir Walter's house last Friday.'

'That's right.'

'Who else was there?'

'Why, there was Alfred Bridson, he's chairman of the constituency party in the City. And Matthew Kimber too. He's the treasurer. Then there was Luke Plowright and Major Applin. They're on the committee because of their family connections, more than for what they do.'

'Is that the lot?'

'Yes, with Sir Walter.'

'You say this was a committee meeting.'

'That's right, just routine constituency business. As you know, the City is solid Tory, and with an election unlikely, there's nothing more important to discuss than garden parties and so on.'

'You'll have a bit more to do now Sir Walter Greville's gone. Who'll replace him? Do you know?'

'The committee will be consulting the various interests

over the next week or so. There's no hurry.' Winterslow's voice held a note of reproof.

'You don't have people waiting in the wings then?'

'No.'

'How long had Sir Walter been a Member for the City?' asked Bragg.

'About two and a half years. He got in at a by-election when Archibald Purdy died.'

'Was he well liked?'

'Why, yes. He was very conscientious. He was at the House regularly when Parliament was sitting.'

'What did he do for a living?'

'He was the principal of Wittrick and Greville, the bankers.'

'Not short of the odd sovereign, then?'

'Rolling in it, I'd say.'

'What kind of a man was he?'

Winterslow pondered for a moment. 'Exemplary is the only word. When he wasn't involved in his political duties, he was working for charity. Open-handed and open-hearted was Sir Walter. A great loss.'

'How did he seem to you on Friday evening?' asked Bragg.

'Just as usual. He wasn't a demonstrative man, you know. Not like me,' he laughed. 'That was one of the best things about him, he was always the same, always calm, always reasonable.'

'So there were no fireworks at the meeting?'

'Indeed no. To tell you the truth, it was very dull.'

'And what happened afterwards?'

'I don't know about the others. I went back home.'

CHAPTER ————— ————— THREE

'Major Applin, please,' said Bragg peremptorily.

The uniformed doorman stared at them appraisingly. 'And who might you be?' he asked coldly.

'Sergeant Bragg of the City of London Police.'

The man sniffed, unimpressed. 'Wait here, and I'll see if he's in.'

The entrance-hall of the club was graced with marble pillars. Between them painted nymphs danced, garlands held aloft.

'Got a fine pair of bouncers, that one,' remarked Bragg. 'Revolts my puritan soul to the core.'

'Very uplifting, I'd say,' replied Morton with a grin.

'Funny sort of places, these. Fancy living in one! Bound to send you barmy, coming home through that massive doorway, and going up those stairs to bed. I expect your

22

parents' place is like this. Explains why you were daft enough to join the police.'

'Good heavens, no! The Priory hasn't got any of this deliberate ostentation. Mind you, from what I've heard the bedrooms here will be very ordinary.'

'Do you belong to a club? The Oxford and Cambridge, I suppose.'

Morton laughed. 'Indeed not. It's in no way compulsory. I always think of gentlemen's clubs as inhabited by public-school boys who've never quite got used to being adult.'

'Whereas you, having only had tutors before you went to Cambridge, are more likely to be found in a lady's boudoir?'

'Something like that.'

'The nearest I came to belonging to a club,' said Bragg with a smile, 'was the hundred and fifty-first Lodge of the Ancient Order of Rachebites! I signed the pledge when I was five . . . with a cross. Some evangelists came to the village, and we all swore our earthly delights away. With me, it lasted till Mary Cartwright's birthday. She was the innkeeper's daughter, and she pinched a bottle of cider . . . Pretty little thing, she was.'

'Major Applin is in the smoking room,' announced the flunkey.

They followed his pointing finger through decorated glass doors into a large panelled room. As they entered, a tall, spare man rose from beside a low table and beckoned them over.

'You're from the police?' he asked.

'Sergeant Bragg and Constable Morton. We're just tidying up our files on the Greville affair.'

'Ah yes. Sit down, won't you?'

His greying hair was cut close to the head, with short side

whiskers, and the ends of his moustache were twisted into waxed spikes. His face had a wooden quality about it. Bragg couldn't decide whether he was mentally dull, or had merely become accustomed to concealing his emotions.

'When did you last see Sir Walter, Major Applin?'

'On the night he died. I was at a committee meeting held in his house.'

'Did he appear in good health?'

'Why, yes.' A shadow of surprise crossed Applin's face.

'We were wondering if he might have had a seizure, which caused him to fall to his death,' explained Bragg.

'I see. No, he seemed just as he normally did.'

'What was your relationship with Sir Walter?'

'I didn't have a relationship as such.' Applin's voice was husky, and his words came out in abrupt bursts, like a seal barking. 'He was one of our MPs, and I helped the Tory Party in the City.'

'You were on the committee, though.'

'True. But I couldn't claim friendship with him.'

'Isn't it odd to find a military man involved in City politics?' asked Bragg.

'Perhaps, but not in my case. My family have strong links with the City. We have a glove factory in Cutler Street. When I retired in 'eighty-six, Alfred Bridson, the chairman, asked me to help out, and I've more or less run the office ever since.'

'What do you do?'

'Write to members, solicit donations, arrange meetings . . . the usual support duties.'

'Did you arrange the committee meeting on Friday?'

'No. It was done at the end of the last one.'

'When was that?'

'The twelfth of June.'

'Including where it was to be held?'

'They've been at Sir Walter's house ever since he became a Member.'

Bragg looked at Applin challengingly. 'So you all knew about the meeting for a month before?'

'And would have been able to predict it much earlier.' Applin's stony face was unmoved. 'The meetings are held on the second Friday of every month.'

'Last Friday there were six of you at the meeting. Did you know that the house was empty apart from yourselves?'

'I didn't know it then,' replied Applin, unruffled. 'And I don't know it now.'

'What did you do after the meeting?'

'I walked back to the West End, had dinner by myself in the Northumberland Arms, off the Strand, and came home to bed.'

'Anyone who can confirm that?'

'I would be surprised if there were . . . unless the doorman remembers seeing me come in.'

'What time was that, sir?'

'I suppose between eleven-thirty and midnight.'

'What kind of a man was Sir Walter Greville?' asked Bragg.

Applin wrinkled his forehead in thought. 'A mediocre man. No particular vices, not really many virtues. He discharged his public duties adequately, but I think without distinction. I cannot speak as to his private affairs.'

'How did he get elected as a Member of Parliament, then?'

'You mistake the nature of politics, if you think that brilliance is required,' replied Applin pedantically. 'The first duty of the City's MPs is to see that its privileges are maintained. At the moment that means fighting off the attempts of the London County Council to absorb it. Thereafter they are expected to support the Tory Party unquestioningly, because that is where the City's interest lies.'

'And Sir Walter fitted that mould?'

'Certainly. He was a City man through and through. His family have been bankers there for generations. He was a dull speaker . . . a dull man really. But he was reliable, and that's what is needed.'

When they emerged, they found that the sky had filled with sudden storm-clouds. The first drops began to fall as they reached the pavement, and soon they were running for the shelter of a doorway.

'Amazing, isn't it,' grumbled Bragg. 'The minute it starts to rain, there isn't a cab in sight.'

'I suppose it will clear the air. It's been very sultry this afternoon.'

The rain was pelting down now, swirling rubbish along the gutters like paper boats on a stream, before sucking them into the Charybdis of a storm-drain. A breathless young woman, her skirt hem saturated, squeezed in beside Bragg.

'You're soaked, and no mistake,' he greeted her. 'Lucky you had your brolly.'

'It's not meant for rain though.' She shook the parasol vigorously. 'It was coming through on to my hair.'

'That's a pretty hat,' Bragg remarked genially, surveying the confection of lace and flowers with a linnet sitting on the top. 'Wouldn't do to get it wet, the bird might drown.'

'Or it might desert its eggs,' chipped in Morton.

'Now you're teasing me,' she said coquettishly. 'There's a hat in Worth's with a real snake coiled round it.' She gave a shiver. 'I couldn't wear that . . . Ah, I think the rain's stopping.' She put up her parasol, smiled brightly at Bragg and took his hand.

'Thank you for looking after me,' she said, and walked briskly away.

'She slipped me a calling-card,' cried Bragg in surprise. '"Virginia Parsons",' he read, '"Fifteen Shepherd Market". That's off Curzon Street isn't it? What's on the bottom? The print is too small for my eyes.'

'You'll have to overcome your vanity, and get some spectacles,' said Morton as he took the small oblong of pasteboard. Then he began to laugh.

'What the hell's the matter with you?' demanded Bragg.

'It's just . . .' spluttered Morton.

'Come on lad, out with it.'

'I . . . I can't . . . It's too funny . . .'

'Nothing's as funny as that.'

'Oh . . . my ribs are aching,' gasped Morton, beginning to laugh again.

'Stop pissing about,' cried Bragg angrily. 'What's on the bloody thing?'

'It says . . .' Morton was shaking with laughter. 'It says . . . "Specially Patient with Older Gentlemen".'

The next morning they ran Luke Plowright to earth in a house in Wakefield Court. A maid ushered them into a sumptuously furnished parlour, the walls covered in pictures, the mantelpiece heavily swathed.

'So you're policemen? What do you want of me?' He threw himself into a chair, and gestured to them to sit.

'We gather you were at the committee meeting in Finsbury Circus last Friday.'

'Yes, I'm on the committee. God knows why. Nobody

listens to what I say. I'm just a dogsbody . . . like old Applin.'

Plowright had bright deep-set eyes and a long nose. With his sallow skin and black hair, he looked unwashed; an impression heightened by the scruffy state of his clothes. As he spoke his lip curled discontentedly.

'The major didn't strike me as old,' remarked Bragg. 'What age would he be?'

'He's a couple of years older than I am . . . say early to mid-forties. What's that got to do with anything, anyway?'

'Just a passing thought, sir. What do you do for a living?'

'I'm a sponger, sergeant.' Bragg looked up questioningly. 'I sponge on my mother.' He gestured with his arm. 'Don't think all this is mine. I've been sold up. My wife and children gone back to her parents. I'm a pensioner of my mother, with no income, and no prospects.'

'I see, sir,' said Bragg cautiously. 'And you help the Tory Party in your spare time.'

'I've plenty of it.'

'Can you tell me what went on at the committee meeting on Friday?'

'I'm sure you didn't come to me first. You must have heard from the others.'

'I'd like to hear it from you, sir.'

Plowright thought for a moment. 'Nothing much. Usual boring stuff. I sleep most of the time. Applin does the minutes, ask him.'

'What would you say the relationship was between Sir Walter and Lady Greville?' asked Bragg, changing his tack.

'A model couple,' sneered Plowright. 'Seemed devoted to each other. Quite the leaders of City society. Used to give lavish parties in that dungeon of theirs.'

'Oddly enough,' went on Bragg, 'I never saw Sir Walter. What was he like?'

'A little squirt. Long body and little short legs. But for his tailor, he'd have looked a freak.'

'I meant, what kind of man was he?'

'Like a lot of small men. Bumptious, self-righteous, ruthless, egotistical, stupid . . . Any and all of those.'

'It sounds as if you didn't like him much,' remarked Bragg.

'I'm a misanthropist, sergeant. You should take no notice of what I say.'

'Very well, sir. Why did they have the committee meetings at Sir Walter's house? Why not at the offices, or at the other Member's house?'

'The office was too cramped, and Christopher Wheeler lives in Islington . . . Couldn't meet out of the City! But the reason was, it gave him extra pull. We met in comfortable surroundings after a generous supper, and we were just a bit more obligated towards him.'

'More than what?'

'More than we were already, with his lavish parties and what not.'

'What was the supper like on Fridays?'

'The usual cold buffet—pickled salmon, guinea fowl, roast beef, a pork stand-pie, that sort of thing.'

'Wouldn't need dinner after that lot,' said Bragg. 'Though you didn't have to eat it, I suppose.'

'When you don't own the price of a saveloy, you eat it all right.'

'And what did you do afterwards?'

'I went to a meeting of the Marine Engineers' Society in Mark Lane, then back here to bed.'

• • •

'Thank you for popping in to see us, Bragg,' called Inspector Cotton in a sarcastic voice. 'It's a great honour for us ordinary policemen.'

Bragg was conscious of Morton beside him, and of the duty-sergeant in the hallway. He walked towards Cotton, in the hope that the inevitable exchange could take place in his room. But the Inspector stood his ground, blocking the doorway.

'How are these enquiries of yours progressing? Have you finished them yet?'

'I am keeping the Commissioner informed of progress, sir, as he ordered.'

'You're supposed to close the fucking thing down, man, not turn it into a full investigation.' Cotton's face was white with anger. 'I could have done all that's needed behind my desk.'

'Yes, sir. Will that be all?' asked Bragg deferentially; then turned on his heel and walked up the stairs.

'That was unforgivable!' exclaimed Morton, when they were safely in Bragg's room. 'What on earth made him act in such a boorish way?'

Bragg filled his pipe carefully and lit it, while his anger ebbed away. 'In some ways these LCC Johnnies are right about the City. It is out of date. We're a perfect example. We're too small to allow everybody who's worth it to be promoted. The senior officers think the bright young men are after their jobs. They're always looking over their shoulders to kick them in the teeth if they get too close.'

'Why don't you transfer to the Met? You'd be a CI in no time.'

'Maybe I'm a snob, and maybe I'm cussed. I'll never get promoted here. I've bent too many rules for that. Anyway I'm right enough as I am.' Bragg puffed at his pipe reflectively. 'Cotton's trying to get me to resign or transfer. That's why he's so bloody-minded. And I have to watch my step, or he'd swing a disciplinary discharge on me as soon as spit. But if I can't win the war, I win the old skirmish now and again.'

CHAPTER ———— ———— FOUR

Bragg stood at his bedroom window, and looked irritably down the street. It had been a hot, still night. He had tried to sleep just in his nightshirt, on top of the bedclothes, but had slept only fitfully. Then, to cap it all, a sparrow perched on the gutter above his open window had kept up an unmusical cheeping since dawn. He'd got up to scare it away once, but it had merely moved out of reach of his flailing arm and started again. He crossed to the mantelpiece and looked at his watch. Still only five o'clock. It seemed to have been light for hours. His landlady, Mrs Jenks, wouldn't be around for another hour. Then she'd have to light the fire. It would be half past six before there'd be any hot water. He rubbed his stubbly chin. Funny how a routine got hold of you. He couldn't ever settle to anything till he'd shaved. Not even when he went back home to Dorset, and was persuaded to go rabbiting with his cousin Jack at first light.

Perhaps he should grow a beard. But nowadays people of his age only grew beards when they got thin on top. He glanced at his speckled reflection in the little mirror above the washing stand. His hair was still thick and dark, with only a few grey hairs. He unhooked the mirror and took it to the window. Looking at his stubble he suspected there would be more grey in his beard than on his head. So that was out. He painstakingly isolated a grey hair in his forelock and tugged. It was surprising how much it hurt. He reached up and hung the mirror back where it belonged. In his newly self-critical mood, he realized that his nightshirt had ridden up over his paunch. He pulled it down with a jerk, but the rounded outline of his belly remained. Well, he couldn't help it. He was a big man, and he was forty-one. It was only to be expected. But if he drank less beer . . . He crossed defiantly to the washing stand and began sluicing his face and neck with cold water. It was tolerable, he decided; even pleasant on such a warm morning. He should be able to shave in it. He gave his razor a thorough stropping, then took up his soap and brush. Certainly it didn't lather as freely as with hot water; it would be interesting to find out why. Still, with a bit more vigour he achieved a respectable lather. By now his damp face was feeling cool, and the touch of the shaving brush was distinctly unpleasant. But as he worked the lather into his beard it warmed up a bit. He dipped his razor into the water and began to shave. He was startled at the difference. A razor dipped in hot water lay on your skin comfortably, seemed to smooth away the bristles. This one was tearing them out. He pulled the skin of his cheek taut, and tried again. It was a bit better, though it wasn't clean, and the lather was rapidly losing its body. He began to scrape his chin, and felt a sharp sting as he cut himself. He swore, and looked around for something to staunch the flow of blood.

A piece of yesterday's newspaper would have to do. He sat on the edge of the bed waiting for it to stick to the cut. Then there was a rap at the door and Mrs Jenks came in with a steaming jug of water.

'A body can't get any sleep these mornings,' she complained, 'with you prowling around above.'

She was wearing a thin wrap over her nightgown, and her hair was in curl-papers.

'Whatever have you been doing to yourself?' she exclaimed. 'You look like a black-and-white minstrel.'

'I thought I'd shave in cold water, and go for a walk,' Bragg mumbled.

'You ought to know better, a grown man like you,' she admonished. 'Why didn't you wake me? I could soon have lit the fire. Now don't let that water go cold, or you'll look like something out of a butcher's shop.'

Bragg smiled at her retreating back. Dora Jenks in curl-papers! Dora Jenks, a widow for ten years . . . much his own age. Who did she do it for? he mused. He was the only other person in the house. Well, well . . .

Morton had scarcely pulled the bell when the door was opened by Lady Greville herself. She looked perturbed.

'Constable Morton, isn't it?' she asked.

'I wonder if I might examine the other rooms of the house.'

She stood irresolute for a moment, then gave a warm smile. 'Of course. It's just that I'm alone in the house today. Ethel is having her day off.'

She turned and mounted the stairs. Morton followed, his eyes on the curves of her waist, made somehow more agreeable by the softness of the black crepe with which her dress was covered. At the landing she paused, hand on her breast. 'I'm always out of breath by the time I get here,' she said with a smile. 'Where shall we start? At the bottom I think, don't you?'

They passed from the top of the grand staircase into a narrow corridor running along the side of the building. Two doors opened from it, and at the far end was a staircase; roughly over the front door. Lady Greville caught his look of surprise.

'Yes, it is odd, isn't it? Walter's grandfather had the house remodelled. He was the first baronet, and he wanted something splendid, I suppose. But it quite ruined what must have been a very gracious building.' She opened the first door. 'This is the dining room.'

It ran along the back of the house. An enormous room, with what appeared to be a butler's pantry beyond it. Two gaseliers hung from the ceiling, above a magnificent mahogany table which looked as if it would seat at least twenty. On the wall opposite the windows was a massive buffet.

'Is this where the committee meeting was held?' asked Morton.

'Yes,' she replied, her face clouding. 'Forgive me. I was trying to forget why you are here. It was silly. I shall have to get used to it.'

'I'm sorry,' said Morton quietly. 'I've had no experience of bereavement. You must feel as if your life has been destroyed.'

'This is the sitting room.' She showed him into a room at the front of the house similar in size to the dining room. It was lavishly furnished, and seemed to belong more in a club or hotel than a private house.

'It's exceedingly cold in the winter,' she smiled.

The next floor was arranged differently again. A corridor ran through the middle of the building parallel to the street,

giving a suite of rooms at the back, and another at the front
of the house.

'My husband had a study here,' said Lady Greville,
leading him into a room overlooking a pleasant walled
garden. 'He used it for his political work. He would write
all his speeches here.' She rested her hand on the small
leather-covered desk that stood by the window. Morton
thought how beautiful she was, with her grave face outlined
against the sky, her unrelieved black dress draining all the
colour from her skin.

'Next to this is his dressing room, then his bedroom and
bathroom,' she went on briskly. 'Do you want to see them?'

'Please.'

'If you don't mind I won't come in with you.'

He casually opened and closed the drawers in the tallboy,
then opened the wardrobe door. On the floor were several
pairs of shoes, none of them bigger than size seven. He
glanced superficially into the bedroom, then turned in
search of Lady Greville. He found her in her boudoir,
staring through the window, lost in thought. In the bright
sunlight, he saw that her hair was the deepest brown, not
black. He crossed towards her, and hearing him she turned
her head. He felt suddenly breathless, as the sun's rays
transmuted the brown of her eyes into a rich amber.

She smiled at him. 'Do you wish to see my bedroom?'
she asked.

Morton felt a blush rising to his cheeks. 'That won't be
necessary,' he mumbled.

'Or the servants' quarters upstairs?'

'No. I've seen enough, thank you.'

She escorted him to the front door, and for the first time
he became aware of the faint perfume of eau-de-cologne.

'Goodbye, constable,' she said. 'If I can help further, I
will do so, of course.'

• • •

Through the open door, Bragg could hear Morton whistling to himself as he mounted the stairs.

'You seem happy, anyway,' he remarked. 'What's the tune?'

'It's the Siegfried Idyll. Wagner wrote it for his wife's birthday. His friends gathered on the staircase early in the morning, and played it to serenade her.'

'A nice thought. Now then, what did you find out?'

'I had a good look at the house. It's furnished luxuriously, and not always in the best taste. Lady Greville says it was remodelled by Sir Walter's grandfather. It sounded as if she didn't want anyone to think she'd had anything to do with it. The living rooms are above the hall we were in, and are much too big for comfort. It must have been decidedly odd for those two living there alone . . . even if there were servants.'

'How many servants are there?'

'Well, it seems as if there's only one at the moment. She said she was alone because it was Ethel's day off.'

'Perhaps she has dailies.'

'The next floor up is on a more comfortable scale. They have two very pleasant suites of rooms, his at the back and hers at the front. Each has a bedroom, bathroom, dressing room and a small sitting room. He used his as a study.'

'So they slept apart did they?' commented Bragg. 'Interesting. I wouldn't have thought she'd mind being slipped a length . . . What's the matter lad?' he demanded. 'Is that too coarse for women of your class?'

Morton flushed. 'She seemed normal enough to me.'

'And what about the shoes?'

'Not above size seven, I would say.'

'What size do you take?'

'Twelves.'

'You know,' said Bragg, reaching for his pipe, 'I don't see somebody with little feet sliding down that staircase like you did. His feet would drop down on each tread, instead of skidding off the edges. And yet he must have been upright when he hit the newel post.' He sucked the flame from the match down into the bowl of his pipe, and flicked it across to the fireplace, leaving a thin wisp of smoke in the air. 'It's amazing how they all see him differently isn't it?'

'Sir Walter?' asked Morton.

'Yes. His wife said he was an aesthete, Winterslow sees him as damned near a saint, Plowright thinks he was a scheming power-seeker, and Applin regarded him as a useful nonentity.'

'Applin was lying yesterday,' interjected Morton. 'I went to the Northumberland Arms to check on his story. In fact the dining room was closed last Friday because the chef was suddenly taken ill.'

'Well, well,' grunted Bragg. 'It looks as if we can't just write it off, whatever the Commissioner would like.'

'You think it was murder?'

'Now don't get excited. We can't say, yet, can we? Applin could have had other reasons for pitching us a yarn. But if we suppose it wasn't an accident, or a death from natural causes, then someone else must have had a hand in it. He certainly seems to have been alone in the house, except for the servants, for quite some time that evening. At least the treasurer and chairman were at the same dinner as Primrose, so they're in the clear. But we should at least check up on the others.'

'Such as?'

'His business associates, the rest of the people at the committee meeting, his wife.'

'Surely you don't suspect his wife? She's heartbroken.'

'You've a funny view of the other sex, haven't you, lad? You think the lower-class women are just for screwing, and the upper-class ones are china dolls.'

'That's most unjust,' protested Morton.

'Maybe. But you'll learn as you get older that they're all just human. I wouldn't like to be in Inspector Cotton's shoes if his wife discovered what he's up to at the moment.'

'Why?'

'She's down in Devon since last Saturday. Their daughter's had her first baby, and Mrs Cotton has gone down to look after her. Pleased as Punch about having a grandson, was Cotton. But it hasn't stopped him going to stay with his fancy piece in Cock Hill, while she's away. His wife's built like a blacksmith. She'd kill him if she found out. That's for sure!'

Wittrick and Greville's bank was tucked behind the Bank of England like a chick with a mother hen. It was a narrow building on four floors, with gothic ornamentation on the façade. Bragg asked to see the manager, and they were shown to a spacious office on the first floor. A distinguished-looking man of about fifty-five rose from behind the desk. He smiled and held out his hand.

'I'm Arthur Hayward. Can I help you in any way?'

'We are tidying up our file on Sir Walter's death, and I felt we should have some idea about the history of the bank and how it worked.'

Hayward smiled affably, and gestured to them to sit. 'Wittrick and Greville is an old-established firm, and for the last hundred years at least has been owned wholly by the Greville family. It prides itself on giving a good old-fashioned service to its clients. It doesn't go in for discounting bills and that kind of commercial business.

Instead it concentrates on giving what select people expect of a bank.'

'How are they selected?' asked Bragg with a show of dullness.

'I mean that the firm is family banker to a few dozen of the best families. We act for the highest in the land.'

'I see. Is it a big bank?'

'Not by joint stock bank standards, but big enough,' replied Hayward frostily.

'You refer to it as a firm,' remarked Morton. 'Is it a partnership, or a company?'

'It used to be owned by a family trust until ten years ago, when it was put into a company.'

'A private company?'

'Yes.'

'Was Sir Walter a shareholder?' asked Bragg.

'As you know, every company has to have at least seven shareholders. Sir Walter held one share, as did five other individuals, but the bulk of the shares were held by the trust.'

'What was the point of the trust?'

'It's very common in banking. Too often the capital of a bank has been dissipated by a wastrel in the family. And, of course, it's better for tax reasons, now we have Estate Duty. Think of paying one per cent on the value of the bank, had Sir Walter owned it personally!'

'What is the bank worth?' asked Morton.

'If you'll wait till the end of next week, you'll be able to see the statutory half-yearly statement.'

'Perhaps you'll let Constable Morton see the last half-year's figures if he calls in a day or two,' interjected Bragg.

'Of course. They are public knowledge.'

'How was the bank run? Did Sir Walter spend all his time here?'

'On the contrary, very little of it. I had to manage the bank's day-to-day affairs, as well as personally conduct the most important business.' Hayward sounded almost petulant. 'He would come down most mornings for an hour or so, and the rest of his time was spent on other things.'

'He was lucky to have you,' remarked Bragg warmly. 'Was he good to work for?'

'He could be a difficult man,' replied Hayward, studying his blotter closely. 'He kept changing his mind. One day he'd tell you to do one thing, the next day he'd say it was wrong.'

'You didn't have the authority to match your responsibility,' suggested Morton.

'That's it,' exclaimed Hayward in surprise. 'That's exactly it. Sir Walter thought he could run the bank in the odd minute he could spare from politics. He was always upsetting the staff. Most of the time they were left to get on with their work. Then he'd call for a file at random, and go through it with a fine tooth-comb. Any little thing wrong and there was hell to pay.'

'Was he by nature a suspicious man?' asked Bragg.

Hayward considered for a moment. 'I don't think so. He was rather pedantic, but I think it was just his way of keeping the staff on their toes. He didn't realize the effect it had on them.'

'Was he a good banker?'

'Not especially. Men born to it seldom are. He was sound, I suppose, in a traditional way, but quite unadventurous.'

'Who dealt with the private affairs?' asked Bragg.

'The trusts and other members of the family were dealt with by me. Sir Walter personally looked after his own affairs, and those of his wife.'

'Can we see his papers, please?'

'You'd better see his private secretary. He knows more about them than I do.' He rang a bell, and a young woman appeared. 'Will you show these gentlemen to Sir Walter's room,' Hayward ordered. 'And ask Mr Pritchard to join them there.'

They went up another flight of stairs to a lavishly appointed office. An enormous partners' desk dominated the room, with leather armchairs on either side of the fireplace. A well-filled bookcase stood against one wall, and the others were covered with maps and prints.

'I don't know what to make of Hayward,' remarked Bragg. 'He seems to have a soft core, somehow. Know what I mean?'

'I've seen something like it in the higher servants at home. They have to make decisions to keep the place running, but they're always unsure of themselves, because their judgment can easily be reversed by someone from the family. There's no finality to their instructions, and everyone knows it.'

The door swung open with a sigh as it touched the deep pile of the carpet, and a young man of about twenty entered. He was tall and slim, with blond hair, and a distinctly supercilious look on his face.

'I gather Mr Hayward suggested you should see me.'

'That's right.'

'What about?' he asked disdainfully.

Bragg looked at him truculently. 'We are police officers. It seems that Sir Walter Greville kept his private papers here. We'd like to see them.'

'They're all locked up in the bookcase cupboard,' replied Pritchard uncertainly.

'Then can we have the key?' asked Bragg, making an effort to achieve a neutral voice.

'Oh, I don't have the key. That was always kept on Sir Walter's key ring.'

'All right, we'll get it tomorrow. Were there any other papers? I can't believe he kept nothing in his desk.'

'Just a few odds and ends. They don't mean anything.' Pritchard opened a drawer, and placed a manilla folder on the tooled leather top.

Bragg flipped rapidly through the contents. They seemed to be mainly receipted rent statements, telephone bills and rate demands.

'What's that?' Morton extracted a small booklet from the pile. 'It's a Giddy and Giddy auction catalogue.'

'Sir Walter bought some *objets d'art* from them, I believe,' explained Pritchard.

Morton glanced through the pages, and found a lot which had been encircled with a thick pencil line.

' "Full set of bronze statuettes of the Plantagenet Kings". Is that what he bought?'

'Yes. He wanted them for the staircase at the house. Paid a tremendous lot for them.'

'I'll keep this if I may,' remarked Morton.

'I suppose it's all right.'

'Do you know what this is about?' asked Bragg. He smoothed a piece of writing paper which had been scribbled on, crumpled up, and then evidently retrieved.

Pritchard peered at it over his shoulder. 'I haven't seen it before,' he replied.

'It's an address, "Fifty-one. Quai de l'Ile, Geneva". Does it mean anything to you?'

'No. I don't think so,' replied Pritchard.

'Go and look in the post book, will you? Let's see if any letters have gone there in the last twelve months.'

Pritchard looked doubtfully at them for a moment, then disappeared.

Bragg glanced across at Morton, absorbed in the catalogue. Now he was a real toff. Son of a general, who was
Lord-Lieutenant of Kent, brought up in a great mansion of a
place that had belonged to the family for generations, and
not a touch of side with him. Not like the little Pritchard
squirt, who was so busy looking down on people he
wouldn't see the birds shitting on his hat. Morton looked up
and smiled.

'If I wasn't a policeman, I think I'd end up as an art
collector,' he said.

And he could too, thought Bragg. He could be anything
he wanted. Wealthy in his own right, handsome enough to
turn any woman's head, a county cricketer, and hence
popular with men, he had with complete perversity chosen
to be a common or garden bobby. When most young men of
twenty of his class would have been frittering away their
time with senseless pleasure, he had been wasting his life in
plodding round the City, trying doors and directing traffic.
An enigma. He'd tried to smoke him out often enough, but
was no nearer discovering why he'd chosen to do it. Still,
he said he enjoyed detective work. Reckoned that was all he
wanted, though it had been rumoured he was being
groomed to be the next Commissioner. Not that he'd shown
any sign . . . but he wouldn't.

Pritchard reappeared. 'There are no entries in the post
book for that address, but if it was a private letter, Sir
Walter might have posted it himself. I've half a mind I
remember seeing a letter from Switzerland marked "Personal and Confidential".'

'When was that?' asked Bragg.

'About a month ago.'

'Did you open it?'

'No. Not with such a superscription.'

'I see. Has anyone come to see Sir Walter from Switzerland recently?'

Pritchard crossed to the desk and took a leather-bound diary from a drawer. 'I'm wondering about last Wednesday,' he said. 'See, the afternoon is struck through, but I'm certain Sir Walter was here.'

'Did you see anyone call?'

'That's the point. He gave me the afternoon off; rather insisted on it, as a matter of fact. He's done that once before when someone was coming to discuss a sensitive matter, and he didn't want me to know.'

'And did you never try to find out who it was?' asked Bragg.

'Of course not,' said Pritchard loftily. 'If he didn't want me to know, I wouldn't dream of prying.'

'What a little squirt that man is,' exclaimed Bragg when they reached the street. 'How does someone like him get into such a position?'

'I would think he's little more than an office-boy,' replied Morton. 'But thanks to him I did get a couple of interesting facts.'

'What are they?'

'You remember he tried to cover the other entries on the page he showed us? Well, I managed to see the entries for Friday the third and Monday the sixth of July.'

'Well, don't keep me in suspense, lad. Get on with it.'

'In the week before he died—before he was murdered, perhaps—Sir Walter had an appointment on Friday with Luke Plowright, and on Monday with Major G. Applin.'

'You saw it clearly?' asked Bragg, his eyes narrowing. 'No possibility you misread it?'

'None.'

'Well, there can't be many people around with names like that. Right, lad. They're expecting you back tomorrow. Go in first thing and have a general look around. Forget the private papers for the minute. See if Applin and Plowright are clients of the bank . . . Blast it!' He swung on his heel and began to walk rapidly back towards the bank. 'That cocky little bugger is making me forget first principles.'

He swung through the entrance doors and made for the girl at the reception desk.

'Back again?' she chirped.

'That's right, my love,' replied Bragg easily. 'You had a caller last Wednesday afternoon. A Swiss chap . . . might have sounded French. Did you get his name?'

'Oh yes, I wouldn't forget him. He could hardly speak English. Had to write his name down before I could get my tongue round it. I have it here, somewhere.' She rummaged amongst the papers in a drawer. 'Yes, here it is. Monsieur Roquebrun. Said he was from Geneva.'

'What time did he come?'

'Soon after I'd got back from lunch.'

'And how long did he stay?'

'Not more than twenty minutes. I remember thinking it was a long way to come for such a short time.'

'What did he look like?'

The girl wrinkled her nose impudently. 'Nothing special. A bit like a copper.'

CHAPTER —————
————— FIVE

Bragg summed Dr Graham up as something of a fop. He was in his late thirties, and so good-looking it verged on the beautiful. His face was clean-shaven, and his crinkly hair was parted in the middle. He wore a modish lounge suit and fashionably knotted cravat.

'You realize I can give you very little information about a patient.' His voice was fairly deep, and had a warm roughness about it. No doubt ninety per cent of his patients were women, most with nothing wrong with them.

'Come now,' replied Bragg cheerfully. 'You're not a lawyer. You can't really claim privilege. A court would force it out of you, so you may as well tell me what little I want to know. Would you say Sir Walter was a healthy man?'

'Yes,' answered the doctor hesitantly. 'The ailments he

has suffered while he has been my patient have been none of them very serious.'

'Are you Lady Greville's physician too?'

'Yes.'

'Does the same go for her?'

Graham nodded briefly.

'Now you were called to the house in Finsbury Circus last Friday night.'

'That is correct.'

'What time was that?'

'I suppose shortly after eleven.'

'And you found the body of Sir Walter Greville.'

Graham nodded again.

'What position was the body in when you found it?'

Graham leaned back in his chair, and gazed at the heavily ornamented ceiling-frieze.

'It was lying on the floor of the hall, quite near the staircase. It was on its left side, I remember, because I didn't see the wound until I turned him on his back.'

'Where was the head, sir?'

'The body was across the foot of the stairs, with the head towards the centre of the room.'

'Where was it in relation to the newel post?'

'Very close to it. There was no doubt in my mind that the injury had been caused by one of those ridiculous carvings on the top of it.'

'How do you think it happened?' asked Bragg.

'There was a loose stair rod near the top of the stairs. It's clear that Sir Walter tripped over the loose carpet, and fell to his death.'

'The loose carpet was on the wall side, though. Do you think, in falling, he could have fetched up against the other side of the staircase?'

'Certainly. It isn't really so wide, sergeant. I think he lurched across to try to get hold of the banisters, and failed.'

'I see. How did you come to find the loose stair rod?'

'Well, Lady Beatrice asked the same question you've just asked me. "How on earth could it have happened?" It was clear he'd fallen down the stairs, so I went to investigate, and found it.'

'Where was Lady Greville when you arrived?'

'She was leaning against the table in a deep state of shock.'

'Who let you in? A servant?'

'No. The door was on the jar, and I left it so.'

'I gather you gave evidence at the inquest as to the time of death?'

'That is correct.'

'When in your opinion did it occur?'

Graham's eyes lifted to the frieze again. 'It must have occurred about an hour before I was called. The body was still warm, and there was no sign of the onset of rigor.'

'It was a hot night, though, wasn't it? Did you take the rectal temperature at all?'

Graham pursed his mouth with irritation. 'That would have been most upsetting to Lady Greville, and was totally unnecessary.'

'I see. Can you describe the wound for me?'

'In layman's terms, the left temple had been crushed in upon the brain by contact with a blunt object. There was some bleeding, but very little. I concluded that death must have been virtually instantaneous.'

'Was the impact on the skull at one point only, or at more than one?'

Graham was beginning to look flustered now. 'I was not able to form an opinion before the coroner came and ordered the body to be moved. But from the way that damned post is carved it could have been either.'

'How was it the coroner happened to come by?' asked Bragg.

'I had him sent for, as soon as I saw Sir Walter was dead. I clearly couldn't sign a death certificate.'

'Of course not. And what time did Dr Primrose arrive?'

'I'd say shortly after half past eleven.'

'What happened then?'

'Well, I showed him the body, and the loose stair rod, and gave him my opinion as to the cause and time of death. Then I persuaded Lady Beatrice to take a sedative, and Dr Primrose said he'd take her to his house for the night. I then left.'

'Were you surprised that there was no post-mortem, sir?'

'I don't know that that is the case,' replied Graham defensively. 'I only know I was called as a witness at the inquest, and gave my opinions as I have given them to you.'

'Would you say they were the opinions of an expert witness, sir?'

Graham bridled. 'I've a considerable acquaintance with death, sergeant.'

'No doubt,' replied Bragg. 'But not many of them violent, I'll be bound.'

'You say you walked from Finsbury Circus to the West End last Friday, had dinner at the Northumberland Arms, and then went back to the club to bed?'

'Right.'

Major Applin was sitting in Bragg's office, very upright, his jacket meticulously brushed, his boots shining. The complete antithesis of Luke Plowright. Morton wondered how they could possibly work together, or indeed what cause could draw them together.

'Would you like to tell us what you had for dinner, sir?'

'Well, I don't see why not.' Applin cleared his throat gruffly. 'Brown Windsor soup, steak and kidney pie, and gooseberry tart.'

'Seems a heavy meal for a warm night,' remarked Bragg. 'Particularly after the supper you had at Sir Walter's.'

'I didn't eat much there, I didn't feel like it.'

'You're quite sure that's what you had for dinner?'

'Of course I'm sure, man,' retorted Applin crossly.

'What would you say,' asked Bragg, 'if I told you that you couldn't have dined at the Northumberland Arms, because it was closed that night?'

'Say? I'd say you were wrong.' Applin glared fiercely at Bragg.

'No. I'm not wrong. We checked up, you see. You didn't expect that, did you? I'll tell you what happened that night,' went on Bragg coldly. 'You left the house with the others, certainly. Maybe you did walk around for a bit, then, as it got dark, you crept back to the house, got inside and murdered Sir Walter Greville.'

An incredulous look crossed Applin's face. 'This is absurd!' he cried. 'I may well be mistaken about the Northumberland Arms, it could have been the next night. I like to stick to a routine. One day is very much like another. I certainly didn't murder Sir Walter.'

'But you did go back. Is that what you're saying?'

'No, I'm not saying that.'

'You couldn't eat the supper that night,' suggested Bragg, 'because you'd already decided that you were going to return to the house, and kill him in cold blood.'

'Absolute nonsense!' cried Applin.

'What was that meeting about?' asked Bragg.

'Surely, sergeant, you haven't neglected to check up on the agenda for the meeting?' Applin permitted a small smile of triumph to cross his lips.

'All right,' said Bragg in annoyance. 'What was it?'

'Apart from the usual routine items, there were three others on the agenda. The first was a report on the accounts for the year to the thirty-first of March; the second was the arrangements for the constituency Ball in the autumn—' Applin paused for effect—'and the third was Parliamentary representation.'

'And the last one was the problem?' asked Bragg.

'Yes.'

'Why put that on the agenda?' asked Morton. 'You had your two sitting Members, and there's no general election in sight. Why discuss Parliamentary representation?'

Applin twirled the ends of his moustache between finger and thumb. 'I'm not really the person to ask about this, because I don't know the ins and outs of it. But it seems that not everyone in the constituency was satisfied with Sir Walter's politics. Some said he was a deal too progressive: you know what a conservative place the City is.'

'So you thrashed it out on Friday?'

'In the event, no. They decided that merely putting the item on the agenda would bring him to heel. Hubert Winterslow moved "Next Business", and the meeting was closed.'

The house in Coopers Row was compact and well-kept. A maid in a neat white apron and cap showed Bragg up to a sitting room on the first floor.

'I'm afraid that my husband isn't at home, sergeant,' said Mrs Winterslow.

'That's no matter,' replied Bragg, accepting the proffered chair. 'I'm sure you can help me equally well. Perhaps even better.'

'I'll try.' She was a faded woman in her late forties, her hair completely grey, and deep lines of worry in her forehead.

'I wanted to get a better idea of the political life in the constituency,' said Bragg smoothly. 'It would help me if I knew more about how Sir Walter and Lady Greville lived.'

'Very splendidly,' she answered somewhat sourly. 'Nobody else could hold a candle to them. It's ironic that I might be the wife of a Member of Parliament, if they hadn't appeared.'

'I thought Sir Walter's family had been here for generations.'

'They have, but he showed no interest in politics till three years ago. When he proposed to stand, Hubert had no chance.'

'Did your husband have reason to think he would be nominated?' asked Bragg.

'It was as good as settled. I wanted Hubert to go on with it, and I know he felt the same for a time. Then he said it was no use fighting against the Greville money.'

'Perhaps you'll be a Member's lady after the by-election,' suggested Bragg.

'The time's gone by for that,' said Mrs Winterslow bitterly.

'Do they have many functions in the constituency?' asked Bragg briskly.

With an effort she dragged her mind from her own troubles. 'They have fund-raising affairs such as the summer garden party and a Ball in the autumn. That used to be all. But the Grevilles have had three or four lavish parties in the course of every winter.'

'What kind of parties?'

'Buffet parties, in that horrid room on the ground floor. It would be full of Ministers and their ladies, all the important men in the Tory Party would be there—and the champagne flowed endlessly.'

'You sound as if you didn't enjoy them.'

'Oh yes, I did. Hubert is very well thought of. I've been introduced to all of the notables . . . It's just that I find such ostentation uncomfortable.'

Bragg eyed her speculatively. 'How did you spend last Friday evening?' he asked.

'Why, I was on my own here, at home.'

'I thought your husband was with you.'

'He didn't . . .' A look of dogged despair settled on her features. 'He didn't come in till the evening was well advanced,' she ended lamely.

'Well, thank you, madam, for your help.'

Mrs Winterslow tugged at a bell by the fireplace, and the maid appeared.

'Good afternoon, sergeant.'

'Good afternoon, ma'am.'

Bragg followed the maid down the stairs to the hall below, then checked. 'I wonder if the cook's in?' he said.

' 'Course, it's nearly tea-time.'

'That's what I thought.'

The maid grinned at him. 'You've got a cheek!'

'You'd stay thirsty without one, on this job.'

'Come on then, but don't you let on. The mistress is real mean. Won't never let me have my boy-friend in.'

Bragg was soon ensconced uncomfortably near a hot oven, with a plate of new-baked scones on his knee and a steaming mug of tea to hand on the corner of the big scrubbed table.

'Is this a good place to work?' he asked.

The cook was plump and big-bosomed. Her face was scarlet from the heat of the fire, and large damp patches were visible around her armpits.

'I've known better. Here,' she said to the maid, 'you can take up the mistress's tray now her visitor's left.' She smiled broadly at Bragg. 'Now you know how tight she is.'

'She didn't seem very happy, I must say,' he remarked.

'I'm sorry for her really,' said the cook. 'The life he leads her.'

'Are they very busy, then?' asked Bragg naively.

'He's busy enough, that's for sure. And if you ask me, with women who are no better than they should be.'

'Really?'

'Well, it stands to reason. Out till all hours of the night. Sometimes he makes so much noise coming in, he wakes the whole house up. Isn't that so?' she demanded of the maid who had now returned.

'Does his wife hear him?' asked Bragg.

' 'Course she does,' asserted the cook. 'She just lets on she doesn't.'

'They sleep apart then?'

'All these rich people do. It's become the fashion,' observed the cook darkly. 'Makes it easier to steal off and sleep with other people, if you ask me.'

'I can't see the mistress stealing off for anybody,' giggled the maid. 'By ten o'clock she's ringing for her cocoa, and off to bed.'

'That explains why she can't remember what time her husband came in last Friday,' remarked Bragg casually.

'Last Friday?' asked the maid. 'He was late last night, I remember. I share a room with the tweenie, and she had toothache, couldn't sleep. There was a dinner on at Trinity

House, and we leaned out of the window watching the carriages coming to pick up the guests. Ever so posh it was. After that Alice kept me awake with her crying. I heard his cab stop, and I got up to look. It was him all right. Very quiet he was for once. I looked at the alarm clock, and it was nearly a quarter to two.''

CHAPTER ——————
—————— SIX

Robert Grumbridge was one of the old school of solicitors. Even in the heat of July he wore a heavy melton morning coat. His shirt had a stand-up collar, and in the knot of his narrow tie was a diamond pin. The corners of his mouth were pulled down, giving him a faintly disapproving air, which was nullified by his chubby pink cheeks and the fringe of white hair round the high dome of his head.

The office had its contradictions also. The room into which Bragg and Morton had been shown was furnished with a heavy mahogany desk and bookcase, thick turkey carpet and velvet curtains at the windows. On a side table was a tantalus with three cut-glass decanters, and matching tumblers in several sizes. By contrast, the outer office had been crammed with cheap desks and clerks perched on high stools; its floor covered with cracked linoleum, where it was visible for the piles of red-taped documents stacked everywhere. Morton supposed the intention was to convince the client that the quality of the advice dispensed by Robert Grumbridge was of the very highest, but that the fees charged—no doubt colossal—were in no way dictated by unnecessarily expensive clerical assistance.

'I see no harm in telling you about Sir Walter's will,' said Grumbridge in a carefully articulated but somehow hollow voice. 'After all, it will be public knowledge within a week.' His hand found the dangling pince-nez and clipped them on his bulbous nose. He then picked up the slim bundle of papers before him, and slipped off the band of red tape. Morton was amused to see that it was the only document on his desk, indeed in the whole room. A client could well believe that he was the only one who mattered to this prestigious firm.

'It is a surprisingly uncomplicated will. After a few small legacies to servants, the sole beneficiary, since Sir Walter pre-deceased her, is his wife.'

Bragg glanced towards Morton and lifted an eyebrow.

'The size of the estate has not yet been determined,' went on Grumbridge. 'However, it is likely to be relatively small.'

'How small?' asked Bragg.

'If I hazarded a guess, I would say it would be unlikely to exceed forty thousand pounds.'

'It seems very little for the head of a banking and landowning family,' observed Morton.

'One might well take that view,' said Grumbridge reflectively. 'There are, however, circumstances affecting this case which make it not at all surprising.'

'Such as?' demanded Bragg.

Grumbridge pursed his mouth in thought.

'Well,' he said eventually, 'all the relevant details are a

matter of public record, or will be in a short time, so I see
no prejudice to my late client's interests in disclosing them
to you . . . You will no doubt be aware that the ownership
of the bank is beneficially vested in a family trust. The
terms of the trust deed defined with some precision the
emoluments which could be paid to the officers of the bank,
and denied to the trustees any power to increase them. As
these limits were set almost one hundred and twenty years
ago, while no doubt munificent then, they are less than
generous now. From time to time the trustees have considered applying to the Court to have the trust varied.
However, it embraces other family interests and properties,
and there was never sufficient agreement among the
members of the family for the trustees to feel justified in
proceeding.'

'But isn't the bank a limited company now?' asked
Morton.

'It is indeed, young man. However, when the company
was incorporated, the restrictive terms of the trust deed
were written into its articles.' He looked at Morton with
reproof. 'A moment's thought will convince you that there
was really no alternative.'

'So how much did he get from the bank?' asked Bragg.

'Three thousand pounds a year.'

'Doesn't seem a bad start to me,' observed Bragg drily.
'What other income did he have?'

'Very little. The other properties were all in the family
trust too, including the estate in Hertfordshire. Sir Walter
was entitled to use that for his own domestic purposes but
he could in no way dispose of it to his personal benefit. The
house in Finsbury Circus was, of course, rented.'

'Presumably Sir Walter had a life interest in the trust?'
remarked Morton.

Grumbridge peered at him over his pince-nez. 'That is so, along with others. This was the crux of the trustees' difficulty. One might be reasonably confident that the Court would have allowed the sale of the estate lands, but there would have been no obvious advantage in applying the proceeds to the purchase of other farming lands. The alternative course would have been to apply them in Municipal Corporation stock, or perhaps in colonial securities. However, the majority of the life-tenants are somewhat . . . er . . . provincial in their outlook, and refused to countenance such a scheme. Without a broad measure of agreement, the trustees felt unable to proceed.'

'Why not invest the money in the bank?' asked Bragg.

'The bank has been somewhat unsuccessful over the past thirty years. It has never attempted to become a commercial bank, like its competitors. It does little more than handle the investments of a number of families and trusts, and provides current account facilities for a diminishing number of individual clients.'

'What do you mean by "somewhat unsuccessful"?'

'Over the last ten years, with the increase in rents and rates in that area, the bank has done little more than wash its own face.'

'So the trust got no income from it?' asked Bragg incredulously.

'That is, alas, the case.'

'And what about the other assets of the trust?'

'They are virtually all agricultural tenancies, and with the decline of agriculture brought about by cheap American grain, the income from them has actually decreased over the last five years.'

'So what has Sir Walter got from the trust?'

'We have just completed his Income Tax return for

eighteen ninety to 'ninety-one, and his trust income for that year was very little over four thousand pounds.'

'With his three thousand from the bank on top?' asked Bragg.

'Correct.'

'And would he have to pay the expenses of the Hertfordshire estate out of that?'

'Only minor domestic expenses. The trust would have discharged all expenditure on the upkeep of the house and its contents.'

There was a silence, and Bragg looked over to Morton enquiringly. The latter decided to voice the question that had been growing in his mind throughout the exchanges.

'Lady Greville is going to be left in a very poor position, isn't she?'

Grumbridge smiled indulgently. 'Well, we don't act for her, but I understand that she is very comfortably off in her own right, under her first husband's marriage settlement.'

'So she's been married before,' remarked Bragg when they were back in the street. 'That's interesting. What's a marriage settlement, lad?'

'You know that in the ordinary way a married woman can't own anything, because all her property is passed to her husband on marriage.'

'It's something that never happened to me!'

'Well, sometimes the bride's family compel the prospective husband to set up a fund under a trust, and if he dies first the fund becomes the property of his widow.'

'That sounds a funny arrangement. Her husband takes over the ownership of her property when they marry, but sets up a fund which will be hers when he dies. Why don't they just let her keep what she had in the first place?'

'Good God!' said Morton with a laugh. 'A suggestion

like that could bring the fabric of society crashing down in ruins . . . The size of the settlement has no relation to the value of the property the wife brings to the marriage. It's really intended to support her in reasonable comfort if she is widowed, rather than become a burden on her own family.'

'I expect you'll find out what it was worth to Lady Greville when you look at the private papers in the bank . . . You know, one of the difficulties I find is that I've no conception of what people at this level spend, to live in the way they do.'

'You should tell Inspector Cotton that you can only do your job properly if they pay you seven thousand a year!'

'Sit down, Mr Plowright,' directed Bragg. 'We're going to follow your advice and take no notice of what you say.'

On his chair in the corner, his pad and pencil at the ready, Morton looked forward to the coming contest with some relish.

'Then I might just as well go away, sergeant.'

'Not until you've made some attempt to give us an unvarnished account of what you know about Sir Walter Greville's death, instead of putting your own slant on it.'

Plowright stared hard at Bragg's impassive face. 'And if I refuse?'

There was a pause. Then to Morton's surprise, Bragg's face relaxed into a broad smile. 'From what you said,' he chuckled, 'we could put you away under the vagrancy acts.'

Morton was fascinated to see an answering smile on Plowright's lips, an implied willingness to proceed on this improbable basis.

'Now we know that you weren't at the Marine Engineers' meeting on the evening of the fourteenth,' said Bragg confidently. 'Partly because it was an all-ticket affair, partly because you're not a member, and anyway because it was held on the thirteenth.'

Plowright laughed sardonically. 'Well, you didn't expect me to put myself on a spit for you to roast, did you?'

'Then what did you do after the meeting, sir?'

'You won't believe me, sergeant, but I walked, by a very circuitous route, back to my mother's house in Bloomsbury . . . I felt the need to work off my irritable mood,' he added.

'I see. And what would you have been irritated about?' asked Bragg.

Plowright's face resumed its usual stubborn look. 'Life in general,' he replied tersely.

'What did you discuss with Sir Walter when you saw him on the third of July?' asked Bragg pleasantly.

Plowright jerked upright in his chair. 'You've obviously seen his notes . . . stop playing with me!'

'Notes can be worded to convey a false impression,' said Bragg, his voice carefully neutral. 'We'd like to hear it from you.'

Plowright glared at Bragg for a space, then relaxed into his chair. 'As you must know, it was a final attempt to get him to keep his word. It was a forlorn hope; I don't believe he ever intended to see it through, the slimy smiling toad . . .'

'Why don't you give us your version from the beginning?' suggested Bragg.

'Perhaps I'm not an engineer,'' Plowright began abruptly. 'But I do know a lot about it. I've an aptitude with mechanical things, I've invented several devices, and patented one or two. But it's difficult to get a manufacturer to take them up.' He looked out of the window in silence for a moment. 'My wife says I'm too easily distracted by a new idea. But a woman would say that, wouldn't she?—they prefer a steady pittance to a chance of real wealth . . . I was one of the first to realize the potential of the dynamo,' he said with pride. 'Most people think of it as part of a boiler house, generating electric light. But if you reverse its function, and supply it with electricity, it will give you motive power. It could be used to drive machines in factories, and horseless carriages as well if it were connected to an accumulator . . . I became deeply interested in electricity, and it was through this that I first met Louis le Prince. He was a Frenchman living in England, and he was doing experiments with moving pictures. Do you know anything about them?'

Bragg and Morton both shook their heads.

'Well, you know the magic lantern, where a lamp projects a picture on the wall? For some years people have been trying to create the illusion that the picture moves. Now if you show a rapid succession of pictures, each slightly different from the previous one, the eye will not detect the substitutions, and it will appear that the picture is moving as if the subject were alive. Fourteen years ago they managed to create this illusion in California by photographing a galloping horse with twenty-four plate cameras. It wasn't completely successful, but when Eastman brought out his celluloid film, it was another piece of the jigsaw put in. I went to America in 'eighty-eight and spent some time helping Edison. We developed a camera using a roll of film, which was passed behind the lens as the shutter opened and closed. In that way you got a succession of pictures each minutely different from the next. The film was pushed along by a sprocket engaging in slots punched in the film. I take some credit for perfecting that.

'Anyway, it seemed to me that the proper course was to reverse the process; just as with the electric motor. Once you'd developed the exposed film, the obvious thing was to pass it through a magic lantern with a similar sprocket. If it passed before the lens at the same speed as it had been pushed through the camera, you would be able to project on a screen that moved just as in life. I say it was obvious, but Edison didn't agree. We managed an experimental projection in 'eighty-nine, but he said you'd never get people to pay for something that only lasted three minutes. Instead he turned it into a glorified peep-show.

'I came back to England in disgust, and shortly after, met Louis. He'd just patented a camera to take moving pictures. I told him what I'd been doing with Edison, and we agreed to work together on a projection machine. Money was the problem, of course, as it usually is. Louis was penniless, I had an annuity provided out of my father's estate. Anyway, I traded on my family's standing in the City, and my acquaintance with Sir Walter, and asked him to support us. At first he wasn't very willing, but by dint of some persuasion, and the promise of political support, he agreed to advance us four thousand pounds. In return he took a charge on my annuity as security.

'We began well. By March of last year we'd patented our designs and started to develop the machine. Unfortunately we had difficulties with the mechanism for advancing the film. The machinists couldn't make it to fine enough tolerances. The film was either held too firmly to the shutter-frame, and broke; or else it wasn't held firmly enough, with the result that it vibrated, the sprocket tore out of the slots, and the whole machine jammed. Because of these difficulties, the money was running out faster than we'd expected. We went to see Sir Walter, when we'd only got five hundred pounds left. I explained what the trouble had been, and told him that we'd found the solution. He promised me that he would support us further, if we needed it.

'Then in June last year, Louis vanished. It was the most incredible thing. He'd been to Dijon to see his parents, and he got on the train to Paris, on his way back . . . and he was never seen again. I kept on with the work, in the hope that Louis would appear again, but by October the money had finally run out. I went to see Sir Walter, and reminded him of his promise. But he said the situation had altered now that Louis was no longer with me. He said he didn't believe I could develop the projection machinery on my own, and he refused to extend the loan.' Plowright paused, and bitterly regarded his scuffed boots.

'What happened then?' asked Bragg.

'Why, the swine called in the loan he'd already made, which he knew I couldn't repay, and took my annuity instead. Nothing I could do about it. I have a wife and two children . . . had them I should say . . . and he reduced me to pauperism. Sold me up, and left me to sponge on my mother. Oh yes, sergeant. If you are looking for someone who would have been glad to see Sir Walter dead, you need look no further . . . Only I didn't kill him.'

Morton put the fragile tea-cup on the windowsill and glanced round the excited gathering in the French drawing room. As Lord Lieutenant, his father was outside politics. So when Lord Salisbury came down to Kent as Prime Minister, rather than as leader of the Tory Party, it was his custom to stay at the Priory. Not that there were any Liberals present as such, but the Sheriff had been appointed by Gladstone during his brief administration in 1886, and the Bishop of Rochester was reputedly almost radical in his views.

The Prime Minister had been punctilious in eschewing party matters. All through dinner he had entertained the company with anecdotes of London society, and vignettes of political figures from both parties. He had refused to be drawn into contentious matters over the port, and had suggested that they might join the ladies with almost indecorous haste. Now he was chatting urbanely to Lady Morton by the fireplace. He was a stocky man, with bald head, fleshy face and a full greying beard. As he talked, his pouchy eyes roved continually round the room.

At least his mother was pleased with the way the evening was going. Morton was always amazed how she had fitted in to English society. Granted her father had been the United States Ambassador to the Court of St James, she had still been brought up in the relatively unrestricted atmosphere of New England. Often enough the difference in background showed: in her direct mode of speech, or her incredulous response to some ingrained English custom. But in the main she had adapted remarkably well, settling happily in to what must have seemed a remote English backwater. He supposed it was the landed interest that was the key. Both her family and her husband's held large estates, attuned to the slow rhythms of agriculture; with labourers, tenants, smiths, dairymaids dependent on them. To marry an English landowner, who was a soldier to boot, and most of the time away on colonial campaigns, must have been a challenge she relished; like a mediaeval chatelaine, or a woman of the American frontier. The former rather, for she obviously loved the old house, and had lavished her own fortune on it unstintingly. She seemed to have an instinctive awareness of the limitations imposed, and the opportunities provided by the Priory's haphazard evolution. As an instance this room, with its heavy gilt mirrors and Louis-Quinze chairs, was lit by two electric chandeliers whose glitter enhanced the gaiety and richness of the scene. In the great hall, where they had just dined, his mother had forbidden electricity. Its austerity was unsullied by such garish modernities, its magnificence rather hinted at by the pools of warm radiance cast by candles in sconces on the linenfold paneling.

Suddenly Lord Salisbury looked across, and beckoned Morton to him.

'I would like this young man to show me the garden,' he announced. 'I'm sure, my dear, your other guests will be impatient that I have monopolized you for so long.'

Lady Morton smiled at her son with pride and curiosity, then slipped away to find her husband.

'These evenings are so warm,' the Prime Minister said as he pushed his way through the French windows. He strolled in silence down the gravelled path, dimly lit by gas lamps that seemed more like Chinese lanterns in the gathering dark.

'I'm told,' he remarked abruptly, 'that you are investigating the death of Sir Walter Greville.'

Morton was nonplussed. 'I didn't know you were aware of it, sir,' he replied evasively.

'The Prime Minister has to be aware of everything that may affect the political scene. He wouldn't last long if he weren't.'

'I wouldn't say that "investigating" was the right word,' said Morton. 'We've been told by the coroner to make discreet enquiries.'

'Some smell of impropriety, isn't there?'

'I'm really in no position to say, sir.'

'Ah well. What I wanted to tell you, is that the Home Secretary will shortly be bringing pressure on the City authorities, and by means of them on the Police Commissioner, to terminate these discreet enquiries. The party managers want to get the writ issued for the by-election, but they wouldn't risk it if some kind of scandal was likely to break out at the same time.'

'I can understand that.'

'Nevertheless, I want these enquiries carried through. We have an ample majority, and much more damage would be done if the Government appeared to be hushing up a scandal.'

'I'll see your views are made known to my superiors.

'Good. But . . ."discreetly", eh?'

'What kind of a man was Sir Walter?' asked Morton.

'Now don't go pushing your investigations as far as the Prime Minister!' laughed Salisbury. 'Oh, he was industrious and predictable; a poor speaker, and without the personal charm to make up for it. But perfect for the City, and thank God not a lawyer . . . the House is full of them.'

'I get the feeling that he was regarded as unreliable in the City.'

'I expect that was his occasional bout of feminism. I think his wife wrote some of his speeches! He used to lecture us sometimes about armies of educated women taking over the offices as they've taken over the hospitals, storming the bastions of the learned professions . . . all nonsense, of course, but certain to raise the temperature of the House.

'It's one of the more amusing incongruities of modern politics,' Salisbury went on. 'Take votes for women. The Liberals claim to be the party of change, particularly the radical faction in it; and the feminists have won over many

of the rank and file. But the leadership, and most particularly Mr Gladstone, is firmly opposed to giving the franchise
to women. On the other hand the leaders of the Tory Party—
myself included—are entirely sympathetic to the aspirations
of women. Unfortunately we are encumbered by a member-
ship which persists in seeing votes for women as a subject
for ribald humour at best. So each party is deadlocked
within itself, and there won't be movement for a generation.'

'At all events, Sir Walter won't be much of a loss?' asked
Morton.

'It's his wife who will be the loss. Have you met her? A
great beauty, and astonishing social flair. Her parties
transformed the political life of the City . . . Yes, we
shall miss her . . .''

Morton was thumbing through a magazine in the small
sitting room when his father came in.

'The PM's gone to bed at last. Care for a whisky?'

'No thank you, sir.'

'Your mother said he collared you and took you out in the
garden.'

'That's right.' Morton glanced across at his father, slim
and erect, a little remote as he had always been, ever
searching for a comfortable relationship with his younger
son, and never finding it.

'She thought perhaps he was suggesting that you should
take up politics.'

'No. I'm afraid it was just about a case I'm working on.'

Sir Henry's face fell. Short of the army, he regarded
politics as the highest form of service. Morton felt it wise to
change the subject.

'Have you ever heard of a Major Applin, sir? George Applin.'

'Hm.' His father sipped his whisky thoughtfully. 'Applin . . . yes, it rings a bell. How old would he be?'

'About mid-forties. He said he retired in 'eighty-six. It seemed to us rather young to retire.'

'Yes, I remember . . . With the Royal Sussex, in India. Resigned his commission. I've an idea there was something unsavoury about it; an enquiry of some sort . . . I half-remember that he shot somebody . . .''

CHAPTER ——————
—————— SEVEN

Bragg brushed some pipe-ash off the front of his jacket, and regarded himself in the mirror on his office wall. If only his eyebrows weren't so bushy. They made him look bad-tempered and aggressive. And his moustache, ragged and stained with nicotine, was positively doleful. He scowled at his reflection, then took up a pair of scissors from his desk and began painstakingly to trim along his top lip.

'Good morning, sergeant.'

Bragg jumped as Morton bounced into the room. 'Be with you in a minute,' he said in embarrassment. 'I never seem to have time to go to the barber's these days.' He looked at the handiwork with dissatisfaction, smoothing the left side down with his fingers to bring it level with the right. 'Enjoy your trip home?' he asked.

'Very much. It was pleasant to get out of this sticky heat

for a while. By the way, I asked mother if she thought the Grevilles could manage on seven thousand a year.'

'Oh yes?'

'It's impossible to tell without knowing the scale of the entertaining; but if the parties were as lavish as you've been told, she thinks they'd have had to count their pennies pretty carefully in between.'

'I can't imagine that, can you?'

'Not from the look of the house . . . Another interesting thing. My father seems to think that Major Applin didn't retire, but resigned his commission because of some scandal in India. He has an idea that Applin shot someone.'

'Now that is interesting,' remarked Bragg. 'I wonder how we can check up on that.'

'He was apparently in the Royal Sussex Regiment. I should think it's more than likely we've got a constable who's served in it.'

'Find out from the office, will you, lad?'

'And most important of all,' went on Morton with an impish grin, 'we're famous! No less a person than the Prime Minister was asking me how we were getting on.'

'Shit! That's all we need.'

'No. You're wrong. He wants us to do it properly.'

There came a rap at the door, and the round, smiling face of Sergeant Griffith from fifth division peered in.

'Joe, I just wanted to remind you about the glee club. We'll be giving a concert in November, and I want plenty of time to polish. You will join, won't you? . . . and this young fellow too, maybe. Do you sing?'

'You bloody Welsh,' exclaimed Bragg grumpily. 'All you think about is singing.'

'Song is the apotheosis of human endeavour. There! Good, isn't it?' He looked at Morton with a grin. 'Got it from a book. Now come on, Joe. You promised you'd join this year.'

'Indeed I did not, Griff. I've told you, Inspector Cotton doesn't care for that kind of thing. He wants his officers free from any commitments, even to their families.'

'Can't you persuade him to change his mind? The glee club reflects well on the police.'

'I've tried,' lied Bragg, 'but it's no use. Mind you,' he went on thoughtfully, 'you could manage it. He likes a spot of flattery, does Inspector Cotton.'

'How do you mean, Joe?'

'Well, Constable Morton here was telling me a tale about some German. Wagner was it?'

'Ah yes, *The Mastersingers*,' nodded Griffith.

'It seems he wrote a piece for his wife as a birthday present, and they played it at dawn outside her window.'

'Sounds marvellous.'

'It's Cotton's birthday next Sunday. What you should do is take the glee club over to his house in the morning and serenade him. I'm sure it will change his attitude . . . but not too early, mind.'

'I'll do it,' exclaimed Griffith with gratitude. 'It'll be good practice for the lads. "Hail Smiling Morn" will be perfect. Where does he live?'

'Cock Hill. Off New Street, by the bonded warehouses. Number five.'

'I've come to see you,' said Winterslow without preamble, ''because Major Applin has told me about your last conversation with him.'

'I see, sir,' replied Bragg unhelpfully.

'It sounds as if we were ganging up on Sir Walter, and that I was the ringleader. But it wasn't like that at all.'

Morton expected Bragg to prompt him, but instead he sat there impassively, his eyes fixed on Winterslow's face.

'You'll find out soon enough that I would have liked to be chosen as the Tory candidate in his place. I admit it. There's nothing dishonourable in that. I've worked hard in the constituency, and I'm well respected in the party generally. I could have done as good a job as him.'

'Indeed, sir,' murmured Bragg.

'But he had an advantage over me that I could never match; and I'm not talking about money. You've seen Lady Beatrice. She was the one that swung it. In three months she had the City eating out of her hand. People I'd been able to count on for years suddenly switched to supporting Greville. And, of course, my wife couldn't come up to her standard. Betty's family were a bit on the ordinary side, and she can't go to a reception without dropping a glass or tripping over her skirt. Anyway, it was put to me that it would be in the party's best interests if I stood aside. It was true enough, so I withdrew. Indeed at the meeting of the selection committee, it was I who proposed Sir Walter as candidate.'

'Were there any other nominations, sir?'

'No . . . The point I want to make is that we were the best of friends. There was no antagonism between us, and I supported him wholeheartedly.'

'Until recently, that is,' suggested Bragg.

'You shouldn't make too much of that, sergeant. All I know is that the view began to form in some quarters that Sir Walter was not in tune with City opinion; God knows why. People began to sound me out, and of course I said I was prepared to serve the party if I was called on. But so far as I was concerned I continued to support him till the day he died.'

'On that day,' remarked Bragg evenly, 'the item "Parliamentary representation'' was on the agenda for the committee meeting. Who put that down?'

'It certainly wasn't me. The agenda is settled by the chairman; though on that occasion I imagine he consulted the other Member, if only to make sure he didn't attend.'

'Major Applin said it was some kind of warning to Sir Walter, to bring him back into line.'

'If it was, then I spoiled it for them, because I moved "next business". Damn it, an MP is entitled to his own opinions, he's not just a puppet.'

'Have you anything else you want to say, sir?'

'No, I don't think so.'

'I called on your wife the other evening,' said Bragg. 'Didn't she tell you?'

'No,' replied Winterslow, his colour deepening.

'You'll be pleased to know that she confirmed all you've just told us about the politics of the City . . . What she didn't confirm was your statement about the time you got home last Friday. You said you went straight home after leaving Finsbury Circus. We now know that you didn't arrive home till a quarter to two next morning.'

'Stupid bitch,' muttered Winterslow to himself. 'All right, sergeant. I admit it. Now you've seen my wife, you won't be surprised I didn't want to spend the evening with her. When I saw how early it was, I took a cab to the West End.'

'And then, sir?'

'I picked up a tart in the parade at the Empire, and went home with her.'

'Where was that?'

'In Soho. Brewer Street I think. I didn't take much notice.'

'What was her name?'

'I didn't ask.'

'Would you recognize her?'

'You know what they say, sergeant. They're all the same lying down.'

'I've found two things so far, that I'd like you to have a look at.'

Bragg and Morton were in Sir Walter's room at the bank, relaxing in the sumptuous armchairs on either side of the fireplace.

'I looked up the index and found that Hubert Winterslow is a client of Wittrick and Greville; or to be more precise, his company is. It has borrowed fifteen thousand pounds from the bank. Here's the file.'

Bragg took the thin manilla folder, and fumbled in his pocket for his pipe; then glancing at his surroundings he furtively put it back.

'The set of accounts on the top is the interesting one,' went on Morton. 'It's a hundred pound company, so all its working capital is provided by the loan.'

'The turnover is certainly high,' observed Bragg. 'But the profit isn't all that great. And all the capital is tied up in stock and debtors. That's the trouble with wholesaling.'

'Winterslow doesn't seem to get much out of it himself, the directors' fees are only two hundred pounds.'

'Oh, he'll have a fat salary up here in the wages entry. It looks a prosperous enough business, as long as you keep on top of the debtors.'

'And so long as the bank loan is maintained,' added Morton.

Bragg pondered for a moment. 'When was the loan advanced?' he asked.

'It seems it was made when the company was first set up.

There is no record of Winterslow's having a loan before then.'

'And when was that?'

'Getting on for three years ago.'

'Hm. It must be very useful to have a bank if you want to get on in politics. Remember what Plowright said the other day? He promised Sir Walter political support if he would finance the magic lantern machine.'

'Do you think the same thing happened here?' asked Morton.

'I'm sure of it. Look how it fits together. Greville wants to oust Winterslow as the next Parliamentary candidate. He's lucky enough to have money, and a charming wife, and he makes some headway. But you're not telling me Winterslow didn't fight back. Of course he did. He's fancied his chances for years. I remember how bitter his wife was. And then suddenly it all fades away, and they're the best of friends.'

'So the loan was a bribe to get Winterslow to bow out?'

'But not just a bribe. It was also a lever to keep him out. Where's the loan agreement . . . Yes, you see? The loan could be called in at any time.' Bragg riffled through the papers. 'Look at this! Winterslow personally guaranteed the loan to the company, and gave the deeds of the Coopers Row house as additional security. So Greville had him properly sewn up. If he stepped out of line, the loan could be called in, and not only would the company collapse, but Winterslow would lose his house as well.'

'Then why was he tempted to be the focus of the discontent with Sir Walter?'

'Why does a moth burn its wings? He could have been a fool, which I doubt, or he could have been a gambler. But suppose he was neither? Suppose he knew there wouldn't be a clash with Greville, because he'd already decided to kill him?'

There was silence in the room for a space, Bragg absently stroking his lopsided moustache.

'I think,' he remarked, 'I would like to know what kind of a man they thought he was in Hertfordshire. Why don't you take a trip into the fresh country air tomorrow?'

CHAPTER ——————
—————— EIGHT

Morton took an early train to St Albans, and secured the
services of a man with a ramshackle dog-cart to drive him to
Fulford. The pony was sturdy and well-groomed, the
morning sunny with a light breeze, and Morton determined
to enjoy his jaunt.

They were soon out in the country, bowling along dirt
roads baked hard by the sun. Although now they trailed a
small stream of dust, it seemed likely that in winter the road
would be muddy and treacherous. Dusky orange depres-
sions showed where the water had stood in puddles. It was
odd that so little attempt had been made to fill them. The
parish was probably too poor to bother. The whole
landscape didn't seem to drain well. Morton could see a
hollow where the ripening wheat was sparse and stunted
compared with the rest of the field, showing that rainwater
had covered it till well into the spring. The trustees of the

Greville family settlement weren't wholly right when they said there was no point in changing land like this. They could easily get better farmland, though it might cost a few pounds an acre more. But bankers or not, the Grevilles would have found it hard to break their connection with this countryside, even if it was a poor investment.

As they breasted a rise, the driver reined in his pony and pointed down into a small valley. 'There's Fulford Hall,' he said.

Some ancient river, much greater than the present docile stream, had smoothed out a wide shallow valley. Its gently sloping sides were wooded, while the floor was covered with close-cropped grass, stippled with enormous oaks and elms. In the middle, partially encircled by a loop of the river, stood a large Jacobean mansion, its warm Cotswold stone glowing in the morning sun. There was no sign of life, not even animals; although the big trees were railed off, presumably to keep deer from nibbling the bark. The sight made Morton uneasy. This had none of the attributes of a working estate. It was a magnificent residence, and with Sir Walter in his grave it seemed to have no purpose.

'Drive into the village,' he directed. 'I'd like to wander around there for a while.'

The centre of the village proved to be little more than a triangle of grass bounded on two sides by low, yellow-brick buildings, and on the third by the churchyard. He strolled across to the smithy, where a perspiring blacksmith was hammering a red-hot horseshoe into shape. In the yard a youth held a carthorse firmly by the bridle. Occasionally the horse would shake its head to clear the flies from its eyes, and the boy would curse viciously. The smith emerged into the sunlight and nodded suspiciously at Morton; then, taking the horse's hind leg between his knees, began to file the hoof with long rasping strokes. Thinking he might find someone more communicative, Morton pushed open the door of the village store. The violent ringing of the bell brought a small girl through the curtain at the back.

'Yes, sir?' she asked diffidently.

'Is your mother in?'

'No.'

'What about your father, then?'

'They're in the top field, turning the hay.'

'Don't worry then. I'll have that pork pie. Cut it in two, will you? . . . And a couple of tomatoes.'

Clutching his paper bags, he walked over the green to the church gate. A couple of rooks flapped from the top of the high elms, and soaring on the diminishing breeze glided away. The church was smaller than he had expected from the height of its spire. The horizontal bands of decaying brickwork between the flint made the walls look squat. There was little or no architectural embellishment, and the whole building was irretrievably earth-bound.

Morton pushed his way through the heavy oak door, and found himself in the cool gloom of the nave. He was surprised to find that there was no stained-glass in the church, not even at the east end. He looked for memorial tablets on the walls, but there were none; no sign of a Greville family pew either. His eyes caught a movement by the altar, and he tiptoed up the shallow stone steps to the chancel. A woman was arranging roses in a large brass vase. At his approach she straightened up.

'Good morning,' she said in a loud proprietorial voice. 'Are you looking round the church?'

'I was an acquaintance of Sir Charles Greville, and I thought I would visit his grave.'

'Oh, that's in the chapel up at the Hall. If you want to see it, you should ask Tom Miller to show you. He'll be around the stables somewhere.'

'Did the Grevilles not use this church?'

'They came down with their guests every Christmas, and often at Easter too. Otherwise they used their own chapel. Old George Greenway, who was vicar here before my husband, acts as chaplain for them.'

'Have they always lived at Fulford Hall?' asked Morton.

'Only for about three generations. That makes them comparative newcomers hereabouts.'

'It's a big family isn't it?'

'I believe so, though there's only an elderly aunt actually living at the Hall now. I expect we shall see some changes soon.'

'Where did Lady Greville come from?'

'Well, of course, she used to be married to John Rawlinson of Shadwell Manor, about four miles from here. I don't know where she was born.'

'They didn't have any children, did they?'

'No.'

'Who will inherit the title?'

'Sir Walter's youngest brother's boy. His father was drowned skating, five years ago. On the whole they don't seem to be a lucky family . . . Ah well, there's a lesson for us all.'

'Will Sir Walter's death affect you?'

'The village, you mean? Not much. All the farms are tenanted, so that will go on as before. And they didn't mix with the village people. I'm afraid Sir Walter was very much an absentee landlord, only coming down here for relaxation. Indeed,' she brightened at the thought, 'if his nephew lives here permanently, it could be a distinct improvement. We might even get our roof repaired.'

• • •

By promising him a half-sovereign, and parting with a moiety of his pie, Morton persuaded his driver to take him to Shadwell. It proved to be a much bigger village than Fulford, lower down the same valley. Here a weir had been built across the river, and the water diverted through sluices to a corn-mill. Morton gave his driver a shilling and, telling him to wait in the Jolly Farmer, sauntered across the road, to where a uniformed police constable stood by the market cross.

'Good day to you. I'm Constable Morton from the City of London force. It's quite a busy little place you have here.'

The policeman looked up sharply, wary of being patronized, but was reassured by Morton's friendly smile.

'From the end of May to now, it's the hay carts getting stuck on the corner there. Then it's the corn lorries coming to the mill. That goes on till spring. If I had my way, I'd knock that corner house down . . . only it belongs to the church.'

'I had to come down to Fulford,' volunteered Morton. 'Sir Walter Greville lived at the Hall, and he died in London.'

'Yes. I heard that. Did you know, his wife used to be married to the squire up at Shadwell Manor? A lovely woman she was, a real lady. No side about her. To my way of thinking, she was better liked than her husband. He was a real Rawlinson. He could hardly bring himself to nod at you if he met you in the road. Mind you, he was a sight better after he got married again. She was his second wife, you understand, and she brought him out no end.'

'I suppose he was a fair bit older than she was.'

'He'd just gone fifty, and she was twenty when they married. By all accounts she could twist him round her little finger. The parties they used to have! And dancing. My Emma used to go and help serve . . . always brought me a leg of chicken or half a pheasant back. And the hunt balls! . . . All the local gentry would come, and plenty of nobs from London.'

'They led quite a social life.'

'Well, that was her, you see. She was one of the Milners from Broadham. A bit of a wild lot. Her father never remarried after his wife died. The children were mostly brought up by the servants. Not that it did her any harm. Many's the time I've seen her galloping across the field after her brothers, and her scarce twelve years old.'

'I hadn't imagined her to be a horsewoman,' remarked Morton.

'The queen of the hunt, she was. Always up with the hounds; hedges, ditches, it was all the same to her. She could beat any man across country. She was lighter you see. I reckon only Tom Barnes, her groom, could hold his own with her; and he was hard as a bone.'

'Not her husband, then?'

'In my opinion, that's what killed him. He would try and keep up with her. And when she was in the mood, she'd jump everything in her way. She used to tell him not to follow, but you know what an old man's like with a young woman. Anyway, one day she was in a real tearaway mood, and she put her horse at a five-foot wall with a drop at the other side. She sailed over it like a bird, but the squire's horse refused. He was thrown straight into the wall and broke his neck.'

'Good God!'

'She never rode again. They say she was near demented. She moved to a cottage in the grounds, and nobody saw her for three months. Her father begged her to come home, but she wouldn't. Then her friends started to visit, and slowly she got over it. Well, it was natural, wasn't it? She was no more than twenty-four, and a real beautiful lady. When Sir

Walter Greville started to pay court to her, you can't blame
her for encouraging him, can you? Good luck to him.'

'Except that he's dead, and she's still not much above
thirty,' remarked Morton. 'She doesn't seem to have much
luck.'

'Ah, Constable Holmes. Sit down, will you? I gather you
served with the Royal Sussex Regiment.'

'That's right, sergeant; second battalion. I'm still on the
reserve for a couple more years.'

'You'll have served in India, then?'

'North-West Frontier, Afghanistan . . . You name it, I
been there.' Holmes was a chirpy cockney, with carroty hair
and a military moustache.

'Did you ever come across a Major Applin?'

'I'll say I bleedin' did . . . Sorry, sergeant.'

'What do you know about him?'

'Well, I can't say I ever really knew him, like. He was in
A company and I was in C. His lads didn't reckon much to
him. Always went by the rule book; he'd never sit down
with 'em for a fag, like our bloke. Didn't last long after he
shot the sailor. It was given out he'd resigned his commission, but everybody knew he'd been given the push.'

'What happened?' asked Bragg.

'Well, there was a tribe on the Frontier called the
Bonerwalls . . . "Bone Wallahs" we called 'em. They
were stirring up trouble at the beginning of 'eighty-six, and
A and C companies of the Royals were sent up to put a stop
to it. We had a detachment of sailors with a Gatling gun, so
I expect General Macgregor thought it was enough.

'It's very rough country, all mountains and steep valleys,
not very easy for infantry. We were always slogging along
the mule tracks, while the tribesmen took pot-shots at us

from the rocks above. You got used to it . . . Anyway old
Applin was senior to our bloke, so he was in command.
Everything went as usual until we were ambushed in a
narrow defile. We took cover behind rocks, and we were
soon knocking 'em down like flies with our new Martini
rifles. But the poor bloody mules were out in the middle,
and after a bit they took off like racehorses down the valley.
Two of them were hitched to the Gatling gun, and they
started off after the others, with the gun swinging and
sliding behind. They hadn't gone far, when it hit a rock,
overturned and dropped into a bit of a hole.

'At that stage, Applin told our company to find a way out
up the side of the valley, so I never saw what happened.
According to one of my mates in A company, a crowd of
tribesmen started gathering higher up the valley. They'd
probably seen us go, and thought they'd charge what was
left of us. Anyway, old Applin suddenly decided he wanted
the Gatling, so he sent for the petty officer in charge of the
naval detachment, and ordered him to take his men and
fetch it. The PO, name of Jackson, by all accounts looked at
Applin as if he'd see him in hell first. None of them could
move from behind their rock without getting shot, and here
was Applin sending them on a job which would take ten
minutes out in the open. Jackson said it couldn't be done,
they'd all be killed before they got to it. Applin repeated his
order as if he was on the parade ground. Jackson looked at
the gun through his telescope, and laughed. You see, he
could tell it wasn't no use going, because the gun was
damaged. A Gatling is a bit like a big revolver, only it's a
cluster of ten .45 rifle barrels that revolve round a centre
shaft. You turn a handle and round they go; and every time
one gets to the top—bang! Well, what Jackson could see
was that the handle was bent right under, so they wouldn't
be able to turn it. As I said, Jacko laughed at him, and

Applin went mad. He ordered him once more to go for the gun. Jackson said there was no point. Applin called him a coward, pulled out his gun and shot him dead.'

'What happened then?' asked Bragg.

'Well, they couldn't hush it up, see. It wasn't one of us he'd shot, it was a sailor; and the navy was hopping mad. They had a court of enquiry. Old Applin said it was "cowardice in the face of the enemy", the navy said it was no more than mutiny; which as far as I can see meant Jacko should have been shot later rather than on the spot. Anyway, the court found Applin's conduct justified. What do you expect? They've got to look after their own, haven't they? But he was shipped back to England, and the next thing we heard, he'd left the army.'

'And now he turns up in the City, and we have a dead politician on our hands,' murmured Bragg.

CHAPTER _____
_____ NINE

'Right, Mr Pritchard,' said Bragg, 'I want to know about everybody Sir Walter saw in the month before his death. Can I have his diary?'

Pritchard stood irresolute, his normally disdainful expression mingled with doubt.

'Come on, lad,' Bragg growled, 'I don't want you to end up as an accessory after the fact.'

Pritchard's eyes opened wide with alarm. 'It's in my room . . . I'll go and get it.' He bolted for the door.

'That was rather wicked, wasn't it?' asked Morton.

'These snobby youngsters get my goat. They know nothing, they don't want to learn anything, and they look down on those that do. See if you can open those windows a bit more, lad, it's sweltering in here.'

Pritchard re-entered, clutching the large leather-bound book. 'Sir Walter always went to Hertfordshire for the last fortnight in June,' he said. 'So he was only back on the twenty-ninth.'

Bragg held his hand out for the diary. 'Good, that cuts it down a bit. Let's see. Nobody in that week till a Mr Plowright on Friday the third of July. Who is he?'

'I don't know. I hadn't seen him before.'

'I shall want the file . . . Did Sir Walter come into the bank at all till the Friday?'

'Yes, every day. He seemed to be looking through files and ledgers.'

'What files and ledgers?' asked Bragg.

'I don't know. He got them himself from the general office.'

'I see. Then on Monday the sixth, there's Major Applin.'

'Sir Walter asked me for the trust folder in the middle of that meeting,' put in Pritchard.

'Let me have it. Then there's Mr Winterslow on the seventh. We've got that file, haven't we?'

Morton nodded.

'Did he see anyone else in that fortnight; apart from possibly the Swiss visitor on the eighth?' asked Bragg.

'He spent all Thursday morning with Mr Hayward,' replied Pritchard hesitantly.

'Right, lad, get the files you've mentioned, and tell Mr Hayward we'd like to see him this afternoon.'

Bragg extracted his pipe and tobacco pouch from his pocket, and took off his jacket. 'Might as well be comfortable,' he remarked. 'We could be here for a long time. Have you looked through the private papers yet?'

'No, I haven't had time. I'll go and get the key to the cupboard tomorrow.'

Bragg dragged the large cut-glass ash-tray towards him and tapped his pipe on its edge. 'I've got to see the Commissioner this afternoon,' he observed, cutting careful slices from a length of twist, and rubbing them between his palms. 'I don't somehow think I shall be telling him what he wants to hear.'

'Your fortnight's not up for some days yet.'

'I know lad, but it can't be done in the time; not this way, at any rate. I feel like a chambermaid, knocking loudly on every door in case I catch somebody on the po.' Bragg began carefully to feed the fragments of tobacco into his pipe. 'Old Primrose will take it he's in the clear with anything short of proven homicide. And when it comes to it, Sir William won't be too happy with a collection of unresolved suspicions. He'll have to take the responsibility for closing the case down, and he's none too keen on putting his own neck on the block.'

Pritchard brought in the files just as Bragg was lighting his pipe, his head enveloped in a cloud of blue smoke. A look of scandalized disbelief crossed his face. He placed the folders on the corner of the desk.

'Is there anything else?' he asked, with a note of disapproval in his voice.

Bragg extinguished the match with a wave of his hand. 'No,' he said without looking up. "Piss off, son, will you.'

Pritchard backed hastily out of the room. As the door closed, Bragg glanced at Morton with a grin. 'Next time he comes in, make sure you have your feet up on the desk.'

'You look pleased with life,' remarked Bragg as Hayward settled himself in the chair opposite.

'I've every reason to,' he replied. 'I have just received a communication from the trustees, intimating their intention of making me a director of the bank. Since I shall be in charge of its operations, I shall in effect be its principal director.'

'At least you've done well out of it. What about the nephew, though?'

'I understand that his interests are more in the agricultural line.'

Bragg picked up a file and opened it. 'We've been looking into the people Sir Walter saw in the few weeks before he died. One of them was a man called Luke Plowright. What can you tell me about him?'

'The other day I said that Sir Walter was unadventurous, but this was one case where he did give financial support to an industrial enterprise.' Hayward scrutinized his fingernails. 'There may have been other factors which affected his decision . . . Mr Plowright's mother comes from an influential City family. At all events, support it he did; in my view for far longer than normal banking prudence would have allowed.'

'Why's that?' asked Bragg.

'The real brains was his partner, a Frenchman, who disappeared last summer. Plowright was nothing more than a tinkerer. He had some inventive imagination, which tended towards what I believe sailors call gadgets. I examined the documents he provided with his loan application. It was true that one or two of his devices had enough originality for him to obtain patent registration, but however ingenious, one could never see them being marketed commercially.'

'People will pay a huckster a shilling for a little round box with yellow pills in,' remarked Bragg. 'So long as they will keep their bowels open, it doesn't matter that they're just made of soap.'

'Ah, yes,' smiled Hayward. 'But that's different. Even in England medicine is largely primitive magic. It doesn't work like that in the industrial field. Let me give you an example. One of Plowright's inventions was a device for extracting corks from wine-bottles. I don't know what you do when you have a cork that's stuck; I just hook the corkscrew round the door handle and pull down on the bottle with both hands. Never fails! Plowright's invention was a mechanical device powered by clockwork. You screwed the instrument into the cork, wound up the engine, threw a lever to release the tension in the spring, and hey presto, the cork was extracted. I suspect, myself, that it would merely tear the centre out of the cork that was really stuck. We shall never know, because Plowright couldn't get anyone to manufacture it. Of course, his claims to have invented a moving picture projection machine sounded plausible enough, and the drawings were most impressive. But if someone like Edison has doubts about a device, one must tread warily.'

'Which was what Sir Walter didn't do,' observed Bragg drily. 'You gave him the benefit of your views?'

'Yes, indeed. As I said, there were probably other considerations. Not that it was long before he began to have doubts. Plowright had very little idea of business organization, and, if you ask me, his whole life was totally undisciplined. I believe that the money advanced by the bank was largely dissipated. Instead of solving their problems on the drawing board, every time a difficulty arose they would have a new prototype machine made. Even if it overcame that particular problem, there were still others they hadn't thought about.'

'For an old-fashioned banker, you seem to know a great deal about engineering,' observed Bragg.

Hayward looked embarrassed for a moment. 'My father was a draughtsman,' he replied.

'So when would you have stopped the loan?'

'I wouldn't have given it in the first place.'

'Nevertheless, Sir Walter seems to have followed usual banking practice, in that he took everything Plowright had.'

'You mean the annuity? It will take us thirty years to get our money back, even ignoring the interest.'

'What about Hubert Winterslow Limited?' asked Bragg, picking up the second file.

'He's a fish wholesaler at Billingsgate. He was Prime Warden of the Worshipful Company of Fishmongers two years ago.'

'Anything special about that loan?'

'They were friends, of course, and both of them active in politics. But it's a prosperous business, and the loan is fully secured.'

'I see. And what about Major Applin?'

'He's the life-tenant of a small trust we look after. He comes in fairly regularly to discuss the investments. If all our clients took as much interest in their affairs as Major Applin, our work would be very much easier.'

'Now, on the Thursday before he died, you spent all morning with Sir Walter. What was that about?'

'That was the usual pattern after a holiday. He would come back full of energy, and start poking into everything. By Thursday he'd collected a pile of files that he wanted to discuss with me.'

'What about them?'

'Trival things in the main. I believe the Plowright case was one of them. He wanted to sell the annuity for a lump sum . . . However, most of the morning was spent in discussing more general matters.'

'Such as?' demanded Bragg.

'He informed me that he was considering withdrawing from the management of the bank. He had realized that his duties as a Member of Parliament left him too little time to effectively direct the affairs of the bank. Further, I gained the impression that he had received intimations of Ministerial office. Sir Walter told me he would recommend to the trustees that I should be appointed a director and manager of the bank, and indeed so it has fallen out. If I evinced any concern when I saw you last week,' he said with a modest smile, 'it was because I feared Sir Walter's death would frustrate my advancement.'

Bragg was surprised, on entering the Commissioner's room, to find the coroner in the chair by the window. He seemed more cadaverous than ever, and he blinked his eyes repeatedly.

'Now then, Bragg,' said the Commissioner. 'I hope you've just about put this thing to bed.'

'I'm making progress, sir, though it's too early to draw firm conclusions.'

'All we want to know is that there was no funny business about Sir Walter's death.'

'I realize that, sir, but I must at least examine all the known factors carefully.'

'So where have we got, then?'

'So far as his wider political life is concerned, I would have no worries. He seems to have been regarded with a kind of indulgent contempt by his colleagues.'

'You needn't bother with that. We all knew him,' broke in Sir William.

'But I didn't know him, sir, so I can look at it with a fresh mind . . . The Prime Minister went so far as to say that Lady Beatrice Greville was more value to the Tories than Sir Walter.'

'The Prime Minister?' exclaimed Summer in astonishment. 'Who to?'

'He was discussing the case with Constable Morton at his parents' home last Wednesday.'

'You've gone too far this time, Bragg,' spluttered the

Commissioner, his face red with anger. 'Who gave you permission to discuss it with anybody outside this office?'

'I gather it was Lord Salisbury who initiated the conversation, sir,' replied Bragg evenly.

'How the hell did he find out? We shall have the newspapers after us next. You know what these politicians are.'

'It seems his intention was to convey to you his desire that a full investigation should be carried out. He is concerned that there should be no suggestion that the truth is being covered up.'

'You're not bulling me, are you?'

'No, sir. He said that you'd be pressed to discontinue the enquiries, because the government wanted to issue the writ for the by-election. His wish was that you should disregard it.'

The Commissioner turned to Primrose. 'It's true, they got a letter this morning.'

The coroner swallowed painfully. 'I would not want to thwart the wishes of the Prime Minister,' he said.

'All right, then, Bragg. What are your problems?'

'The underlying difficulty is that we are expected to believe that Sir Walter fell down the stairs, and hit his head on the carved newel post hard enough to kill him. He wasn't a tall man, I'm told, and he would have had to be upright for his head to be in the right position. That might have been possible if he hadn't fallen far. But the loose stair rod was at the top, and he must have fallen so far, for his skull to be crushed. For my money, by the time he got half way down the stairs he would have been sliding on his back or his front.

'Having decided I wasn't convinced about the cause of death, I began to wonder if there was anyone who could benefit from his death. His family seem to be excluded. He has no children, and his wife has an independent fortune of her own. More particularly, he isn't a very rich man, as any of his relations would know. All the family's wealth is tied up in a trust.'

'Who else would want him dead?' demanded Sir William.

'I can think of at least two people who might. Both of them on the committee of the constituency party. A youngish man called Luke Plowright admitted he would have liked to see Greville dead. It seems he regards him as the author of all his misfortunes. But he denies murdering him, naturally. The second is Hubert Winterslow.'

'Winterslow? Don't be stupid, man. He's a leading figure in the City. They were tipping him as a likely MP a few years ago.'

'You are right, sir. That's the cause of the trouble. Sir Walter came on the scene with his money and his charming new wife, and all Winterslow's supporters deserted him. He was forced to give way, which he wouldn't do willingly. He's a fighter is Winterslow. He says they were the best of friends, but I don't believe it. I think he was lying low, biding his chance. Not that it would come easily. Sir Walter's bank had financed a big expansion of Winterslow's business, so they had him by the short and curlies. All this had happened three years ago, of course, but there was a new element. Some people were dissatisfied with Sir Walter, and were trying to persuade Winterslow to stand against him at the next election. With his business and house mortgaged to the hilt, the only way it would have been possible was with Sir Walter dead.

'Both these people had the opportunity to kill him,' went on Bragg. 'They had been at the committee meeting that evening at his house, and either of them could have gone back and killed him.'

'Could either of them prove he didn't?'

'Not in my judgment, sir. One of them spent the evening walking round the West End, the other was with a prostitute in Soho.'

'So where are we, Bragg?'

'I'm not satisfied it was an accident, sir, but proving it was murder is a very different matter. The evidence of the doctor who examined the body is, in my opinion, not to be relied on. Our next move must be to have a proper post-mortem examination carried out by an experienced police-surgeon.'

There was a gasp from the coroner. 'If you applied for an exhumation order,' he wavered, 'I would have to resign.'

The Commissioner appeared not to have heard him. The uncomfortable silence seemed to prolong itself into minutes. Then he leaned forward. 'Is that what you are asking for, Bragg?' he demanded truculently.

'Yes, sir. As to the coroner's position, the burial took place in Hertfordshire, so the exhumation would be well away from the City. I'm sure Dr Primrose could arrange for Dr Burney to do the post-mortem up there. We could have the pathologist's report very quickly.'

'No doubt the Home Office would agree, to oblige the Prime Minister,' said Sir William with heavy sarcasm. 'Very well, Bragg, you'll get your order.'

CHAPTER ———— ———— TEN

The sun was already dazzling as Bragg and Morton walked quietly along New Street, though it still lacked a few minutes to seven o'clock. Since it was Sunday morning, the streets were deserted. Back in Bishopgate they had seen a solitary milkman, his float weighed down with churns; but otherwise no one. Morton suspected that people had revelled in the comparative cool of the previous morning, and were sleeping late.

Bragg turned into Cock Hill, a long terrace of two-storeyed houses, and motioned Morton to keep to the wall. They tiptoed past the door of number five, its paintwork stained with bath brick around the gleaming brass knocker.

'Quick!' murmured Bragg. 'Across the road into that alley.'

They scampered across like schoolboys, and found a shadowed doorway which gave them a good view of the

house. The upstairs window had been flung up at the
bottom, but the curtains were still closed.

Bragg consulted his watch. 'Come on Griff,' he muttered. 'They'll be getting up before long.'

'If Inspector Cotton's wife is coming home next week,
they may lie in,' whispered Morton. 'Make the best of
today.'

'I'd take her on a boat trip to Margate if I were him, not
lie in a frowsty bedroom all day . . . Ah! It looks as if
something is happening.'

Two or three uniformed policemen appeared briefly at the
entrance of Cook Hill, peered around, pointed, and withdrew.

'They'll be gathering just round the corner,' remarked
Bragg smugly. 'Won't be long now.' He hauled his watch
out of his pocket again, then nudged Morton and pointed
down the street. A group of about twenty policemen, their
uniforms carefully brushed, their buttons glinting in the
sun, crept along the opposite pavement, and assembled
beneath the bedroom window. An excited Sergeant Griffith
gestured and pushed, until they were in a rough semi-circle.
Then licking his thumb, he distributed a sheet of music to
each man. There was some shuffling, as self-conscious
grins were exchanged, and Griffith looked up at the window
anxiously; but all remained quiet. He raised his hand for
attention, then taking a tuning-fork from his pocket, flicked
it with his fingernail and held it to his ear. Morton heard him
hum an arpeggio, which was taken up by the choir until a
soft chord resounded in the street. He could see Bragg's
teeth bared in a fierce smile, as Griffith's hand slashed down
on the first beat.

'Hail smiling morn, smiling morn, smiling morn.
That tips the hills with gold, that tips the hills with gold.'
There was a rattle from above as the curtains were drawn

back, and the blonde head of a scantily clad woman peered out of the window. She smiled and waved at the singers, then looked over her shoulder and beckoned. Griffith returned her smile, and encouraged the choir with ever more imperious waves of his hands.

'At whose bright presence darkness fla-a-a-a-ies away
Fli-ies away-ay, fla-a-a-a-ies away.'

The blonde head was withdrawn, and replaced by that of Inspector Cotton. He took in the scene below, and exploded in anger.

'What the bloody hell are you doing?' he cried.

His words were drowned by the chorus. Griffith glanced upwards, and catching sight of the Inspector, flailed his men on. By now windows up and down the street were opening and heads appearing.

'Fla-a-a-a-ies away, fli-ies away-ay.'

'Get out of here!' shouted Cotton in a frenzy. 'I'll have you all arrested! You there, what's your name? . . .'

For a moment the choir seemed to be holding its own against the furious shouts from above.

'At whose bright pres-ence . . .'

Then a slight uncertainty set in, and the diminution in sound allowed the cries to gain the upper hand.

'Go away! I'll bloody have you for this!'

The back rank of the choir, seeing the wrathful face of the Inspector, began to shuffle away. Griffith lashed about him, singing desperately to keep it going. Then panic struck, and the men began to run down the street after their fellows. Griffith, in an effort to salvage something from the disaster, saluted smartly in the direction of Cotton.

'Happy Birthday, Inspector,' he called, then hurried after the choir.

'You'll bloody pay for this!' cried Cotton as he slammed the window shut.

Hearing the thud, the men stopped running, and gathered around Griffith, tittering guiltily.

Bragg allowed an ecstatic chuckle to escape his lips. 'Perfect,' he murmured. 'Couldn't have done it better at the Tivoli.' He turned to Morton. 'You see what I mean, about winning the odd skirmish. There'll be the devil to pay tomorrow, but by God it was worth it!'

Catherine Marsden sat at her dressing-table brushing her hair. The unbelievable excitement she had felt when she'd been accepted as a junior reporter on the *City Press* had still not subsided. Even though it was only published twice a week, and concerned itself mainly with the esoteric affairs of the City, it was a real newspaper. And she had a real job, with as much pay as a man would get. She allowed herself to feel a little smug. With the exception of one or two doctors, there were very few women could say as much. Doubtless Daddy had helped in some way or other. Completely lacking in experience, she would never have been accepted without some intervention on her behalf. Perhaps he had painted a more than usually flattering portrait of the paper's owner! Still, the great thing was to grasp the opportunity. She smiled as she recollected her interview with the editor. He had been at something of a loss to describe her duties. The idea seemed to be a small column which would interest women readers. Catherine suspected they could be counted on the fingers of one hand; indeed she couldn't imagine any woman avidly reading the *City Press*. Perhaps she could change that, at least so far as her contribution was concerned. And even if she couldn't make women buy the paper, she could at least represent the woman's point of view. The editor had mumbled about social and charitable functions, as if they were the only proper concern of women, and then added something about home-life and children. Well, she wasn't an authority on either of those subjects. She was an only child, and had long ago decided that her home-life had been distinctly untypical. Her father had always been something of a socialite, not just to ensure a continuing supply of commissions, but because he enjoyed it. Her mother, on the other hand, was charming in a vague, disorganized way; but she was more interested in Hardy, with Thackeray for light relief, than the day to day concerns of running a household and bringing up a child. Indeed she had seemed almost overawed by her exuberant and assertive offspring. When her father complained that their daughter would never get a husband, she would wave a hand ineffectually and say: 'I'm sure she could, if that was what she wanted.'

Well, that was true enough, thought Catherine, looking at her reflection in the mirror. If men were stupid enough to set prettiness above intelligence, that was their loss. At the moment she had far more important things to do than think about young men. She coiled her back hair up into a bun, skewered her hat on her head, and calling goodbye to her mother, stepped out into the warm sunshine.

She had a presentiment that today was going to be exceptionally important, so she decided to take a hansom instead of the omnibus. If her interview went well, she would certainly make her mark with the piece she would write. Perhaps the *Star*, or even *The Times* would be clamouring for her services. As they turned into Old Jewry she banished the fantasy and took hold on her mounting excitement. The way to get on in a man's world was to control emotion, and let the head rule.

'Inspector Cotton?' repeated the desk sergeant. 'Yes, he's expecting you.'

The Inspector stood as she entered. She got the impression of a handsome man in his late forties, well-preserved, and of intimidating bulk. She felt herself smiling at him in an ingratiating way; not at all the cool self-confident approach she had planned. He seemed surprised by her appearance, and was appraising her with a blend of avuncular geniality and concupiscence. At least, she thought, I don't look too unattractive.

'I'm very pleased to meet you,' he said, taking her hand. 'It's encouraging to have the press taking an interest in the police force.'

'Are you in charge of the detective division?' asked Catherine, getting out her pad and pencil.

'Let's say I'm the senior Inspector, shall we?' said Cotton with a smile.

'And what are your responsibilities?'

'I head the largest section of the division, with probably the most experienced men under me.'

'I've seen your name occasionally in reports of Old Bailey trials.'

Cotton preened himself. 'I've had a certain amount of success in the kind of case that interests the public,' he replied modestly.

'But you don't carry out the actual investigations yourself, surely?'

'No, no. I become involved at an advanced stage, when it's clear from the evidence that there will be a prosecution. The way evidence is given can be a crucial factor in securing a conviction.'

'You mean that your men gather the evidence, but you appear in the witness box?'

'The most experienced men would give their own evidence, unless, that is, the case were very complicated or there were other good reasons. Naturally,' he added, 'the detectives would get full credit for the work they had done.'

'Are not the men disappointed when they can't give evidence in a case they have worked on?' Catherine asked with a smile.

'Not at all. We are employed for the protection of the public, not their entertainment.' Cotton paused to allow Catherine to record his *bon mot*, and she deliberately prolonged it to prepare for a switch of tone.

'You gave evidence in a case last week, at the Old Bailey.' She pretended to consult her notes. 'A man called Michael O'Hara.'

'That's right. Giving false information to the Registrar of Deaths.'

'You directed the investigations leading to his arrest?'
'Correct.'

'Would you tell me about the case?'

Cotton settled back in his chair. 'It was a bare-faced attempt at fraud on an insurance company,' he began expansively. 'You have to know that in some types of life assurance policies, when premiums have not been paid, the policy is taken back by the agent, and treated as lapsed. That doesn't mean that it's cancelled, it's just suspended. If the policy-holder's circumstances improve, the arrears of premium can be paid and the policy revived. Now O'Hara had access to medical certificates of death, probably stolen. He approached an agent of the Prudential, and struck a bargain with him. The agent would give O'Hara some lapsed policies, and they would pay enough premium to revive them. Then O'Hara would get a forged medical certificate of the death of the policy-holder. He would take this to the Registrar of Births and Deaths, get a death certificate, and use it to claim the insurance monies under the policy. Very ingenious.'

'How many times had they done this?'
'Just the once.'

'At what stage did the police become aware of the crime?'

Cotton looked up sharply. 'At an early stage,' he said dismissively, the bonhomie gone from his voice.

'Isn't it true to say that the agent contacted by O'Hara went straight to his head office?'

'I believe it is, why?'

'And that someone from the Pru came to see you?' Catherine persisted.

'That is so.'

'What was the outcome of that meeting?'

Cotton frowned. 'I really can't disclose the subject matter of confidential discussions.'

'And yet the result of that consultation with the police was that the Pru provided their agent with a lapsed policy on the life of a young woman called Lumley. Is that right?'

'I've told you, I cannot say.'

'You presumably aren't suggesting that the Pru didn't come to you for advice, or that you didn't give it?'

Cotton glared at Catherine without replying.

'At all events, it appears from *The Times* report that O'Hara, posing as Mrs Lumley's father-in-law, produced a medical certificate of death to the Registrar, and was given a death certificate. I think you gave evidence as to that in the court?'

'Yes,' said Cotton briefly.

'And he then claimed the insurance monies and was arrested. You see,' she went on in a reasonable tone, 'the difficulty I have is that the police were aware of the possibility of a crime long before any crime was committed. Now I know that the police are charged with the prevention and detection of crime, but as a journalist it seems to me that here the police were actually procuring the commission of a crime in order to arrest O'Hara. Would you agree?'

'Of course I don't agree,' said Cotton irritably. 'He's a rogue, and he's in gaol where he belongs.'

'And his wife and children are begging in the streets,' said Catherine bleakly.

'What's that to do with me? I'm here to uphold the law.'

'But if O'Hara hadn't been given the policy, he might never have committed a crime at all.'

'He would. He's a wrong 'un, I tell you.'

'That's what worries me about this case, Inspector. On the basis of the discussion between O'Hara and the insurance agent as to how they might defraud the Pru, you seem to have decided he would be better behind bars. You in fact trapped him into committing it by giving him the policy, and were standing by ready to tap him on the shoulder.'

'Are you saying we should give these villains a fair chance, or something?' asked Cotton with a sarcastic laugh.

'I'm saying that it's Star Chamber justice to assist in the commission of a crime and then arrest its perpetrator.'

'What do you know about it? At the very least he was guilty of conspiracy before we appeared on the scene.'

'I don't think that can be right,' observed Catherine thoughtfully. 'A man can't conspire with himself, and there's no evidence that the insurance agent ever agreed that they should together use O'Hara's plans to defraud the Pru. No, the only agreement between them came after you had told the Pru to provide the policy.'

'Look, miss,' exclaimed Cotton wrathfully, 'why don't you go and pester somebody else? There's a damned sight worse going on right under your nose. You ought to find out what Sergeant Bragg is up to. Yes,' he smiled, as he watched her jot down the name. 'Detective Sergeant Bragg and Detective Constable Morton, two of my own men, and I'm not allowed to know what they're doing.'

• • •

By the time Bragg and Morton had walked to Finsbury Circus they were regretting it. There had been a change in the weather. Instead of the clear blazing heat, there was a haze over the sky, a brooding stillness as if the sun had sucked all the earth's moisture into the heavens and was holding it there suspended. Not that there were any clouds; the sun was a glowing yellow disc in the east, and the temperature was if anything even higher than the previous day's. Morton had changed into a lighter lounge suit, but despite that he could feel a trickle of perspiration between his shoulder-blades. Bragg was still wearing his old morning coat, and now and again he would take off his hat and mop his head with a handkerchief.

'Sergeant,' ventured Morton.

'Yes?'

'I've been picked to play in Kent's match against Gloucester in the first week of August.'

'Oh?' remarked Bragg grumpily.

'I would like to play . . . and you know I missed the Notts match.'

'Look lad, I know they think you're somebody special because you can knock a little leather ball over the wall at Lord's. I might not agree, but most times I would go along with it. But this case is special too, and till it's cleared up, the arrangement for you to play cricket is cancelled. Right?'

Bragg hammered on the door of number nine and after a few moments it was opened by the housekeeper.

'Good morning, Mrs . . .''

'Shorter.'

'We're back again.'

'Well, come in then,' she replied irritably. 'I'm trying to keep this place cool.'

'You must have known Sir Walter very well,' remarked Bragg, closing the door after them. 'How long have you been here?'

'Never set eyes on him. I've been here exactly two weeks today.'

'Really? What about the cook, then?'

'Same with her. We both came from an agency soon after he died.'

'Do you live in?'

'I do. Cook doesn't. Mind you,' she added, 'I've got a room of my own in Paddington. You've got to when you're doing agency work.'

'Why don't you take a permanent position?' asked Morton.

'I prefer a change,' replied Mrs Shorter briefly.

'What other servants are there?' asked Bragg.

'None to speak of. I even have to do cleaning myself, and that's never happened to me before.'

'Surely you have help?'

'Only one cleaning woman coming in daily . . . and she's new too, in case you want to know.'

'I see. Is her ladyship in?'

'Wait here.'

'She's in a bad mood today,' remarked Bragg at her retreating back. 'How many servants do you think it would take to run this place?'

'It would depend on your style of living,' replied Morton. 'But just to keep it clean would take three or four maids, and a housekeeper. If you were going to live well and entertain guests, you'd probably need a cook and a couple of kitchen maids as well.'

'A small army, and all to provide for the needs of two people.'

'You sound disapproving, sergeant.'

'I suppose I am . . . Don't get me wrong. I pulled the forelock as hard as anyone when I was young. It didn't do me any harm either. But it was different in the country, it was like a family and you knew your place in it. Here it's all just done for money. Take that Shorter woman. She's not bothered that Lady Greville's just been widowed, she's more concerned that she's been asked to do a spot dusting . . . though what there could be in the houskeeping line at the moment, I don't know. I don't suppose Lady Greville thinks tuppence about her servants either, probably sacks them if they break a cup.'

Morton was about to disagree, when he remembered the look on her face as he'd brushed the dust from his coat.

'Lady Greville will see you,' announced the housekeeper. 'She's in her boudoir. She said Constable Morton knew the way.'

Bragg raised a challenging eyebrow at Morton. 'Sounds as if you've been doing some investigating on your own account.'

She received them with a sad smile, the warmth of her eyes accentuated by the shadows of grief under them.

'We've called for the keys to Sir Walter's cupboard at the bank,' said Morton kindly.

'Ah yes. You'll find them in his bedroom, I'm sure. Perhaps the sergeant would like to look over the house, while you are here.'

Morton found a bundle of keys in the top drawer of the tallboy, then showed Bragg Sir Walter's study and bathroom. Coming back down the corridor, he was conscious of the fragrance from Lady Greville's bedroom. When they returned to the boudoir she was standing in the window staring out at the gardens in the middle of the Circus, and fingering a string of jet beads around her throat.

'Did you find them?' She turned, and again her eyes glowed amber in the sunlight.

Morton nodded.

'We were surprised to hear that all the servants were new,' remarked Bragg.

'Why is that?' she smiled.

'I would have thought you would want things to remain the same for a bit . . . to help you get over it.'

'That's thoughtful of you, but you see it wasn't possible. I shall not be able to keep on the house myself, and I gather that the trustees have no need of it. I'm told that the lease will be up in a month.'

'Where will you go?' asked Morton.

'I'll probably find a small house in Kensington or St James's; something more suited to my reduced income and my widowhood.'

'But why discharge them only two days after your husband's death?' persisted Bragg.

'As it happens, I knew that Lady Gore was looking for a cook and a housekeeper for her Belgravia house, so I sent Alice and Mrs Roberts along to see her. I gather she's delighted with them. You know how difficult it is to get really good domestics. As to the maids, in all honesty, sergeant, I couldn't bear to have them in the house again. It was the carelessness of one of them that was responsible for my husband's death, though naturally none of them would own up to it.'

'I understand, ma'am,' said Bragg sympathetically.

'Have you completed your enquiries, sergeant?'

'I'm afraid not. These things tend to drag on.'

'Poor Walter,' she said, her lips trembling. 'He was such a dignified man . . .'

'I'm sorry ma'am,' said Bragg quietly. 'We'll get through it as soon as we can.'

'She's going through a difficult time,' remarked Morton when they were back in the street. 'I don't think she ought to be on her own. Why doesn't she go back to her family?'

'If she did, we'd have a long way to go to talk to her!'

'Isn't she beautiful, though? Did you see her eyes?'

'Yes. Very striking they are . . . remind me of black treacle.'

'Black treacle?' laughed Morton incredulously.

'You know, when you have it on your knife it's a dark brown, but when you spread it on your bread and butter it becomes all tawny. I don't expect you've ever done it, you poor deprived devil.'

Major Applin came down to the smoking room to meet them. There was a certain jauntiness about his walk, and he seemed almost pleased to see them.

'We have learned that you, or rather a trust in which you have an interest, is a client of Wittrick and Greville,' said Bragg.

'That's correct, sergeant.'

'We also know that on the Monday before he died, you spent the morning with Sir Walter Greville. Why didn't you tell us before?'

'I didn't think it was of importance,' replied Applin.

'What did you talk about with Sir Walter on the sixth?'

'I saw him in connection with the trust. I've always taken an interest in the way the funds are invested; I like to keep on top of them.'

'But this wasn't a routine meeting. I gather from Sir Walter's private secretary that it went on for two hours.'

'That's perfectly right. For some years, the trust fund has been invested wholly in securities—Consols, debentures, some Canadian loan stock. On the last statement of trust assets, which I received on the third of July, I discovered that some of the Consols had been sold, and replaced by property and equity shares. Now I know that the interest on Consols isn't sparkling by any means, but it is safe. So naturally I wanted to know why the changes had been made.'

'And did you find out?'

'No. They had been done on the instructions of the manager, Mr Hayward, and he was out with a client. Sir Walter and I looked through the file, but we couldn't find anything except a schedule of assets identical to the one I had received.'

'I see. Can we go back to the committee meeting on the tenth? We took your advice, and went to see Mr Winterslow about the agenda. He says that some people were asking him to stand against Sir Walter, if there were an election. Did you know about that?'

'I'd heard rumours.'

'I gather the meeting that Friday was not particularly friendly; one might even call it acrimonious.'

Applin pursed his lips. 'There were some suggestions of bad faith, it's true, but I would prefer not to discuss what still seems to me a completely private matter.'

'You needn't think we shall let go,' said Bragg. 'We're only just starting. It's going to be done properly, as it should have been right from the start.'

'You're going to exhume him!' cried Applin excitedly. 'When? Could I come and watch?'

'You shouldn't jump to conclusions, sir,' Bragg admonished.

'The funeral was so solemn and pompous in that little chapel of theirs. It's droll to think of you spiriting him away at dead of night to cut him up.'

'You were at the funeral, sir?'

'Oh yes. We all went along to pay our respects.'

'If you ask me,' remarked Bragg as he and Morton passed through the hall, 'everybody who knew Sir Walter had remarkably little respect for him. Surely even in England money alone can't get you so far?'

'Excuse me, are you Sergeant Bragg?' A young woman was barring their way. She was dressed in a severe blue costume, a stiff collar and jabot, and a small feathered hat.

'I am, miss.'

'My name is Catherine Marsden. I'm from the *City Press*.'

'Oh yes?' replied Bragg non-committally.

'You were at a house in Finsbury Circus this morning.'

'Were we?'

'Yes, you were, because I followed you there.'

'And how did you know to follow us, may I ask?'

'I can't tell you that.'

Bragg looked at her speculatively, and said nothing.

'The house is occupied by the widow of Sir Walter Greville, who died there a fortnight ago. Is it true that there are suspicious circumstances surrounding his death?'

Bragg sighed in vexation. 'What does a good-looking young woman like you want getting mixed up with these grubby newspaper folk? They're not your kind. You'd be better off at home with a baby on your knee.'

The girl flushed. 'Patronizing me won't help. The only way you'll get rid of me is to answer my questions.'

'Well, I suppose it will be a change to be followed about by a lady of no doubt impeccable virtue, eh lad?'

'Is it true?' repeated the girl.

'All I can tell you is what's on the public record.'

'Which is?'

'Oh, so you haven't had time to do your homework? That's interesting. Never mind, I'll tell you. Sir Walter

Greville died on the tenth of July. On the thirteenth of July an inquest was held and the verdict was accidental death. The evidence was that he fell down the stairs.'

'And did he?' she asked.

'I expect so.'

'May I ask who you've been seeing in the club?'

'Now, one of your less virtuous sisters wouldn't need to ask. She'd know how to find out herself.'

For a moment there was a look of pure hate on the girl's face, then she turned, hesitated, and walked into the club.

'I've a strong suspicion,' remarked Bragg heavily, 'that our little caper yesterday may cost us dear.'

CHAPTER ELEVEN

Morton knocked on the door of the mews cottage, and after a few moments it was opened by a sprightly old lady. She was wearing a trim skirt and blouse, and a white lace cap was perched on her silver hair. Her only concession to infirmity appeared to be the crocheted shawl around her shoulders. She invited him to sit down, and settled in her rocking chair with obvious pleasure.

'Do you have many visitors?' he asked.

'Never enough! Lady Bea comes to see me most days, but often that has to last me till the next day. Now my eyes are getting old I can't read much, and the days are so long.'

'You were Lady Greville's governess, weren't you?'

'I was. I was practically her mother too. Poor little thing was only five when her mother died. Her father should have married again, to give those children a proper home. She was growing up more like a boy than a young lady, when I took charge of her.'

'How old was she then?'

'Just gone twelve. She really ought to have gone to a girls' boarding school, but her father couldn't bear to be parted from her. He used to ask her opinions about things as if she were his dead wife. Not that he treasured her memory. He used to carry on shamefully with all the women of the neighbourhood, but I didn't think he ever really cared for them. "I can trust my little Bea with you," he'd say to me, and off he'd go; sometimes for days on end.'

'What happened about her brothers?' asked Morton.

'Oh, I didn't have anything to do with them. He professed to be seeing to their bringing up himself. He sent them to the local school, and left them to their own devices. I fear Mr Milner didn't have much time for education.' Her mouth pursed disapprovingly. 'Still, that was his affair. I think the most he ever did towards their upbringing was to beat them regularly, whether they deserved it or not. Mind you, they generally did deserve it. They were a pair of real harum-scarums if ever I saw one. In summer the trap would hardly stop before they'd have thrown in their satchels and be off round to the stables for their ponies. They were hard boys, those two, and they've grown into hard men. Charles, the elder, is a captain in the Royal Artillery now.'

'Lady Beatrice was fond of horses too, wasn't she?'

A suspicious look flitted across the old face. 'Yes, she was a good rider,' she conceded after a pause. 'She could keep up with her brothers any day. But I didn't encourage it. My task was to turn her into a young lady, and a hard time she gave me for the first couple of years. Then suddenly she changed. It wasn't just growing up; most girls change at that age, but they generally get more difficult. My Bea was the opposite; she became as docile as I could wish, and couldn't learn too much.'

'What caused it?' asked Morton.

The old lady smiled secretly. 'I think she just discovered she was beautiful. I couldn't understand it, and then one night when she'd gone to bed early, I crept up after her and peered in. There she was, mother-naked in the lamplight, looking at herself in the mirror . . . And she was beautiful, soft smooth skin without a blemish on her, and those innocent brown eyes. Mind you, she could be a monkey too. By the time she was seventeen, she was more or less running the house for her father. Woe betide a servant who was lazy or careless! . . . She could be self-righteous, too, at times. She once reported the local bobby to the Watch Committee for wearing his uniform while he was worse for drink.'

'He doesn't seem to have held it against her,' said Morton with a smile.

'Well, she was told that uniform or not, he wasn't on duty at the time, so she rode straight over and apologized to him. Fancy apologizing to the local bobby! But she was like that; as generous as could be, when the mood struck her.'

'I still don't know how you managed to turn this tomboy you've described into the charming lady I met the other day,' observed Morton.

'I can't take a lot of credit,' said the old lady with a rueful smile. 'She mostly did it herself. She started to read every novel she could get hold of. She'd have two or three out of the lending library every week. The Brontës were particular favourites, but the one she used to like most was Mr Disraeli. She would quote *Coningsby* to me by the yard.'

'You wouldn't imagine a young woman liking political novels.'

'No, but she always had a serious cast of mind under it

all. And, of course, it has stood her in good stead these last few years.'

'Have you always been with her?'

'Ever since I set foot in her father's house. "Emmy," she would say—my name's Emmeline Hewitt—"you'll always have a home with me, even if you are old." Bless her! I was all of fifty-five at the time. But she's been as good as her word.'

'So you were with her at Shadwell Manor?'

'Yes.' Again there was the hint of restraint.

'She became a very experienced hostess, I gather, during her marriage to Mr Rawlinson.'

'Oh yes. They had lots of parties, but not like here. Do you know, we've had the Prime Minister to dinner here . . . many a time.'

'How did her first husband die?'

'I was away at my sister's at the time . . . a riding accident, I believe.'

'Lady Beatrice never discussed it with you?'

'Bless you, she was a grown woman then. She didn't discuss things with her old governess.'

'What do you do when she comes over to see you now?'

'Why, it's mostly in the evenings, and we just sit and chat about old times.'

'How long does she stay?'

'She doesn't like me being on my own at night, so she generally stays till we hear Tom come in, and then goes.'

'Who is Tom?'

'He's the coachman. He has the room above this.'

'Is that Tom Barnes?'

'Yes.'

'He's always been with her too?'

'Yes. He's supposed to look after me, and see I'm all right, but I can manage perfectly well by myself.'

'Do you remember what happened on the night Sir Walter died?'

'Nothing different from usual. If anything we sat even longer, it was such a beautiful evening.'

'What time would you think she left?'

'I couldn't say exactly. It had been dark a good long time.'

'And you didn't hear any disturbance from the house?'

'No I didn't,' she smiled. 'Praise be to God, I sleep like the dead.'

'Can I have your working files on the Applin trust, please?' asked Morton.

Hayward looked up blankly.

'I asked the chief clerk if these were the only papers on the trust, and he said you would have the working files in your cupboard.'

'I'm sorry, my mind was elsewhere. Yes, I'll have someone look them out for you.'

'I'd like them now, please.'

Hayward looked about to demur, then relented and began to pull files from the cupboard. 'Here they are,' he said.

Morton withdrew to Sir Walter's room, and laid the contents of the two files out on the desk. They bore out what Applin had said. There was a note of each purchase or sale of an investment, together with the relevant contract note. Regular lists of the investments, together with their values, had been prepared, and each bore an annotation 'Copy to GA' with a date. He also saw that there had been recent purchases of shares and of property. The shares were seven separate parcels in different trading companies, and in each case the business had been valued by the same firm of accountants on a going-concern basis. The property comprised a row of leasehold houses in Rotherhithe Street on the south bank of the Thames. This, too, was supported by a valuation.

Morton was about to replace the papers in the files, when he noticed a number pencilled on the top of the property valuation. He took the sheet down to the general office. 'Is this some kind of reference number?' he asked.

'Yes. Every investment we make is listed in the investment register,' explained the chief clerk cheerfully, 'and given a number.' He crossed to a cupboard and took down a large black ledger. 'Let me see . . . Here we are; a row of houses in Rotherhithe Street. You see, it works!'

'What is this entry for?'

'In that column we record where we purchased the investment from. In the case of a publicly quoted stock we would put the name of the stockbroker. Then if it's sold, we note where it goes in this column.'

'The entry in this case says "see IL 1587",' remarked Morton.

"Then if we look up line 1587, we shall see where it's come from.' The clerk licked his finger, and rapidly flicked through the pages. 'Here we are . . . The property was transferred from T 114, which should be a trust.' He darted across to a desk and took a register from a clerk. 'T one one four,' he muttered. 'Yes, it came from the Compton Settlement.'

'Can I have the file?'

'Of course.'

Morton had been cursorily reading through the trust deed for some minutes when he realized, with distaste, that Lucy Compton must have been the mistress of a titled gentleman, and the trust had been set up to care for her and her bastard child. The sum settled had been enough to produce an adequate income to keep them both in reasonable comfort.

But on the death of Miss Compton, or her marriage, the capital was to revert to the settlor; unless her daughter was still alive and unmarried, in which case she in turn would enjoy the income until marriage or death. Morton felt a revulsion from this careful drafting of a family lawyer, and the underlying lack of generosity in the settlement.

'You're looking sour,' said Bragg as he poked his head round the door.

'Just looking at this settlement. It's a trust set up by a scion of a noble family to get rid of an inconvenient mistress and her child.'

'Well don't look down your nose at it. She probably prefers it to being in the workhouse. How does that concern us?'

'Some property and equity shares have been transferred out of it to the Applin Trust.'

'Are these the transactions the major was talking about yesterday?'

'Yes, they were all transferred on the twenty-first of May.'

'I wonder why.' Bragg peered over Morton's shoulder. 'Here's a letter from some firm of solicitors out in the sticks, dated the fourteenth of May. It's suggesting that there should be a valuation of the trust assets. Are they trustees, or something?' Bragg seized the deed. 'Yes, you see, the senior partner of the solicitors, and the bank are trustees of the settlement. Has there been any correspondence with the firm before?'

'There's none I can see.'

'It looks to me that a new partner got hold of the file and decided to stir it up a bit. Now why should that cause these assets to be transferred to Applin's trust? There's no connection, is there?'

'I wouldn't think it was conceivably possible. We could ask Hayward, I suppose.'

'No. Hayward caused the transfer to be made. I'd rather know the answers before I talk to him about it. Rotherhithe Street isn't far. Make a note of the address, and we'll go and look.'

They took a cab, and clattered over London Bridge, past the railway station, and along the backs of the wharves. Before long they entered the western end of Rotherhithe Street, in a seedy area of low-class houses. The roadway became progressively more filthy, and the houses more dilapidated, until rounding a bend, they found the road blocked by a corrugated iron fence.

'Hello, what's this?' cried Bragg.

'The houses we're interested in should be the second or third block beyond the fence,' said Morton.

They got down from the cab and peered over the fence. The nearest houses had their windows boarded up; the next block was in the process of being demolished.

'Of course,' said Bragg, 'they're levelling the site for the new Surrey Docks. Now that raises one or two interesting propositions. Number one, Hayward must have known the houses were just so much hard core, and transferred them out to avoid detection. Number two, Major Applin could have discovered it as we did, so his meeting with Greville might not have been the cosy affair he made out. Number three, if we're right about them, then Greville's chat with Hayward was nothing to do with leaving him to manage the bank on his own . . . Interesting isn't it?'

'And suddenly,' said Morton thoughtfully, 'we seem to have two more people who might prefer to have Sir Walter dead.'

CHAPTER ——————
—————— TWELVE

Bragg and Morton had picked up Dr Burney at the Golden Lane mortuary. With his hamper of specimen-jars strapped on top of the growler, they looked as if they were off on a picnic in the country. No doubt the onlookers regarded it as the utmost folly, for the steamy heat of the past fortnight threatened to break in thunder. All the afternoon there had been a growing tension, a realization near to a hope that there would be an orgastic storm to wash away the foetid stickiness, and allow life to return to normal. As they swung into the forecourt of St Pancras station, the clock struck six. Morton glanced up at the tower, silhouetted against the leaden sky, like a vast cathedral dedicated to some barbaric rite.

The train was packed with clerks going home to Kentish Town or Hampstead. Dr Burney persuaded the guard that he must stay with the hamper in the guard's van. Bragg and

Morton forced themselves into a crowded compartment, receiving a vicious look from the man who had up till then expected to be at the window. By the time the train started, the heat was intense, and even with the windows down there was little ventilation because of the press of people. To make matters worse, a man lucky enough to have a seat began to smoke some disgusting black shag in his pipe. For ten minutes Morton was wondering what he could do, wedged in as he was, if his stomach finally revolted. Then the train miraculously emptied, and Dr Burney, discovering he could abandon his jars after all, joined them.

'I find it's always better to travel in the guard's van during rush-hour,' he said with a smile. 'I hope you've brought your capes. It always seems to rain harder and wetter in a churchyard than anywhere else on earth. I've got a gamp in the hamper there.' He had a cherubic face and a wide, loose mouth. He appeared to live in perpetual delight, for he would screw up his eyes and smile whenever he spoke. It was, thought Morton, a welcome contrast to the tetchiness that had beset Londoners of late.

'I suppose you can't tell me what this is all about?' Burney beamed.

'Through some oversight of the coroner, no post-mortem was done when Sir Walter Greville died,' said Bragg. 'We aren't very happy with the evidence presented to the jury at the inquest, so we want you to have a look.'

Burney cocked his head. 'Are you by-passing the coroner?' he asked.

'No. Dr Primrose specifically asked that we should carry out the enquiries.'

'I knew Greville had died, of course,' went on Burney. 'I imagined that the police-surgeon for the first division must have taken a look. Who gave the medical evidence at the inquest?'

'The family doctor.'

'Well, well! . . . The coroner's being squeezed, naturally. Is it political?'

'Not to my knowledge,' replied Bragg.

'Internecine strife is splendid entertainment, if you can stay out of the ring,' pronounced Burney.

'Don't you fancy being the next coroner?'

'Not I! Where is the interest in sitting on a dais pontificating, instead of getting your hands in? Would you give up detection to sit behind a desk? Anyway, I'd have to resign my chair at Bart's.'

'Why, then, at least we'll be able to assume your report is unbiased, won't we?' said Bragg straight-faced.

'Sergeant Bragg,' replied Burney genially, 'I hope that when I come to do an autopsy on you, I shall find . . . that you're not quite dead.'

At St Albans they were met by a sergeant, and six uniformed constables complete with pickaxes and spades. They crammed themselves into a wagonette brake drawn by two horses; Morton sitting at the front with his feet on Dr Burney's hamper. Before long they were out in the country, following the road that Morton had traversed the previous Friday. Now the stillness was oppressive, the muffled thud of the horses' hooves on the hard clay seemed a puny challenge to the heavy silence. After half an hour the driver had to stop to light his lamps, so deep was the gloom. As Morton looked up, he could see ragged drifts of cloud, themselves lighter than the rest, being driven across the sky by some high-level wind. Occasionally he felt a great drop of rain. He caught a glimpse of Fulford Hall, dark and forlorn in its valley.

When they reached the village they took a narrow road at the side of the church, and soon found themselves running by a high brick wall. This was evidently the boundary wall of the estate, for it circumscribed a rough curve round the back of the Hall. They passed an imposing gateway flanked by two lodges, and about half a mile further on stopped at a narrow entrance closed by a wooden farm gate. The sergeant clambered down and knocked on the door of a small cottage nearby. An old man in clerical garb came out, holding a lantern high.

'I'm Mr Greenway, the chaplain here,' he said. 'It has fallen to my lot to assist at this sad business.'

'Where is the graveyard?' asked Burney.

'It's over there, about half a mile away,' replied the chaplain, gesturing across the field.

'Can't we take the wagonette closer?' asked one of the constables irritably.

'I'm afraid not. The only drive to it comes from the house.'

'Doesn't this road go to the house?' asked another.

'It's never used. You'll have to carry your things across the field,' replied the chaplain sharply, and set off purposefully over a stile.

There was a murmur of discontent as the constables extracted tools and canvas screens from under the seats, and set off across the tussocky pasture.

'I hope this isn't going to be much heavier on the return trip,' remarked Morton, as he hoisted the hamper to his shoulder.

'Only enough to keep me off the rough end of the coroner's tongue,' replied Burney. 'Talking of which, I see the police have got a new scourge for their backs.'

'What's this?' asked Bragg.

'You haven't seen the hit in today's *City Press*, then? An account of an interview with your Inspector Cotton about a fraud case. Very cleverly written. Left you in no doubt that the police had the man set. They seem to have helped him with the crime, then arrested him. I suppose it improves your rate of apprehensions, but it sounds a bit sharp, a bit too Frenchified for my liking.'

'That's not like the *City Press*,' said Bragg.

'Apparently they've got a new reporter . . . a young woman they say . . . ended up with a bit about the wife and homeless children. I should think Cotton won't be best pleased.'

'If that's the case, we can expect problems. We've had one brush with her ourselves. I reckon Inspector Cotton set her on to us . . . Ah, here comes the thunder.'

The sky was now black overhead, and lightning flickered along the horizon. In the light from the flashes they became aware of a wall ahead of them. It had been built out from the boundary wall to enclose an acre or so, and through the iron gateway they could see the headstones of graves.

As they caught up with the rest of the party, there was a sigh in the trees around, a sudden crack of thunder, and the rain began to patter down. The chaplain hurriedly undid a rusty padlock, and pushed open the gate.

'Which grave is it, sir?' asked the sergeant, with the briskness of someone who would not be wielding a pickaxe.

'Oh, Sir Walter's in the mausoleum, not in a grave,' replied Greenway.

'Bloody hell!' grumbled a constable. 'What have we brought these spades and things for?'

'That's enough,' barked the sergeant. 'You men, stay outside. I want Smith and Cox inside with me.'

Greenway led them to a low chapel-like building at one end of the graveyard. The door opened easily on its hinges and the light from the lantern revealed a flight of stone steps leading down into the blackness.

'Smith, Cox, bring the other lanterns,' called the sergeant.

Morton groped his way down the stairs after Greenway and found himself in a large chamber, half underground. In the flickering light, he could see that the walls were lined with three rows of deep granite shelves. Along one side, they were stacked with coffins as dust-grey as the granite itself. At the extremity of the pool of light they seemed to move eerily, as the shadows danced in the lantern-light.

'Christ!' exclaimed Smith, as he led the others down. 'I never seen anything like this afore . . . Gives me the creeps.'

'That's the one.' Greenway pointed to a gleaming ebony coffin on the other side. 'There are some trestles at the end, there.'

Morton, the sergeant and the two constables took hold of the coffin, slid it from its niche and stood back reverently.

'Right, where's my box?' cried Burney zestfully. 'Constable, will you put a lantern on the shelf, and another opposite . . . on that coffin will do . . . splendid! Now, sergeant, can we open him up?' The policemen looked at each other doubtfully. 'Screwdriver, screwdriver! Surely you've brought one?'

'Ah, yes sir. Prior's got one, hasn't he, Cox? Give him a shout.'

Prior, young and dim-witted, got half way down the stairs and stopped, white-faced.

'Come on, give it to me,' said the sergeant irritably. Prior lunged down the steps, dropped the screwdriver in the sergeant's hands, and fled. 'Here you are, Smith, you used to be a joiner, get the lid off.' Smith took the screwdriver, and with a strained look began painstakingly to remove the long brass screws. Finally he stood back with a sigh of relief. 'That's the lot.'

'Well, what are you afraid of?' exclaimed the sergeant, and gesturing at Smith, seized the top end of the lid and raised it. At that moment there was an echoing crash of thunder above, a gasp of horror from the sergeant, and a clatter as the coffin lid dropped to the floor.

'Oh my Gawd! It's not got no 'ead,' he cried.

Burney, startled, peered into the open coffin. 'Goodness me!' he exclaimed. 'Presumably he wasn't buried like that. I'm sure all his loving friends and relations saw him screwed down . . . Here's a pretty problem for you. Sergeant Bragg.'

'Applin,' muttered Bragg. 'He guessed we were going to have a post-mortem. When did we see him?'

'Monday,' replied Morton.

'That was quick work. Is it as recent as that, sir?'

'I'll have to take a closer look,' replied Burney. 'Here, you men, lift the coffin on to the floor, and put the lid on the trestles . . . the inside upwards . . . that's right. Now lift the body on to the lid.' He grinned at the startled faces of the constables. 'There may be a little liquid in the bottom, but it won't harm you.'

With the corpse precariously balanced on the coffin lid, Burney took a lantern and examined the stump of the neck. 'It's been embalmed, of course, so it's difficult to be precise. But I'd say it's not been off more than a day or two . . . probably with a large pocket knife, say a four-inch blade. Done very roughly . . . no anatomical knowledge, I'd say. See where he's hacked at the vertebra here . . . probably pressed for time, too. Ah well,' he smiled, 'might as well take a look inside.' With Smith's reluctant assistance he removed the shroud. Then taking a scalpel, with a sweep of his arm he opened the torso from neck to crotch. A look of revulsion crossed the sergeant's face.

'Let's see if we can find the head,' he suggested. 'Smith, you stay and help the doctor.'

They took a couple of lanterns, and, splitting up into pairs, began to stumble about amongst the graves, half blinded by the driving rain.

'Mind you,' grumbled Bragg, 'it's not likely to be here. He'd hardly go to all that trouble and just drop it behind the nearest gravestone.'

'Saturday is the earliest it's likely to have been done,' mused Morton. 'because that was the first time you mentioned exhumation to anyone.'

'You mean it needn't have been Applin? I suppose you're right. I imagine the Commissioner had a letter sent to the Home Office Saturday morning, and the coroner couldn't be relied on to keep his mouth shut, the state he's in. Lots of people might have known before the major . . . And, of course, Applin might have given the news to someone else . . . Perhaps we'd better not jump in with both feet. An arrest would get the papers humming all right. Any luck, sergeant?'

'No. We'll have a proper search in the daylight, but I doubt we'll find it. Here, come and have a look at this.' He led the way to the gate and removed the iron chain which secured it. 'See, one of the links has been prised open. That's how he got in . . . and they don't lock the chapel-place, the reverend says.'

'Right, boys,' called Burney from the vault. 'I've finished. Help me tidy up, and we can go home.'

They replaced the body in the coffin, and a white-faced Smith screwed back the lid.

'I've got a few goodies to take back with me,' observed Burney with a smile. 'But from my examination here, and bearing in mind the embalming, I would be surprised to find any evidence of disease. I haven't, of course, examined the head.'

'And whoever cut it off,' said Bragg grimly, 'knew it

would tell us very plainly how Sir Walter died. We're not farting about any longer. This is a case of murder.'

By the time they had lugged their equipment back to the brake, they were saturated. Oddly enough this seemed to lift their spirits, as if the rain trickling down their necks was a welcome relief from the oppressive heat. One of the constables joked about the tinkle of bottles from the hamper, and Burney replied that he was welcome to the spirit in there, though he might not find it to his liking. Occasionally a crunch of thunder overhead would frighten the horses, and they would lay their ears back and falter till the driver cracked his whip at them. Here and there the road had turned into a stream as the rain ran off the rock-hard fields. Once they had to get out and push the brake up an incline, because the surface of the clay had become a slimy film that gave the horses' feet inadequate purchase. By the time they reached St Albans it was a quarter to twelve, and the last train to London had gone. They took their leave of the local sergeant and his men, and gained possession of the empty waiting room. At first they accepted their enforced vigil philosophically, and Bragg smoked a leisurely pipe. After an hour or so, however, their wet clothes began to feel clammy as the temperature dropped.

Bragg shivered. 'It's worse than night duty,' he said.

'You'd better take care,' admonished Burney. 'You could catch your death of cold.'

'Not with you around, surely? You'll fix me up with something.'

'Good heavens, no,' exclaimed Burney in alarm. 'Never go to a doctor if you're ill. Doctors kill more patients than they cure. I should know. I've not been to a doctor for twenty years. The best thing for a cold is half a tumbler of brandy with a little hot milk in it, as you go to bed. If it

develops into a cough, rub your chest with goose grease.
Better than all your doctors and fancy medicines.'

'It sounds revolting,' said Morton with a laugh.

'Maybe, but it works. You try it next time!'

For the time conversation languished. Bragg propped
himself disconsolately in the corner, and Morton stretched
out on the hard wooden bench. Then there was a rattle at the
door, and a porter entered. He looked at them with surprise.

'Hey, you can't sleep here,' he cried in a hoarse voice.
'Off you go to the workhouse.'

Burney enfolded him in a beatific smile. 'We are not
vagrants, my man. I am Professor Burney of the University
of London, this is Chief Inspector Bragg and this Inspector
Morton, both of the City of London Police. We have missed
the last train, and are compelled to spend the night in your
not very salubrious waiting room. I suggest that you should
get some blankets and sandwiches, and endeavour to make
us comfortable instead of ejecting us.'

The man regarded them with interest.

'You here on a case?' he asked.

'That is correct.'

'What's it about?'

'You'll read about it in the papers.'

'I'll tell you what,' said the porter, looking at his watch.
'I'll get the signalman to stop the mail-train. You'll be in
London by three.'

CHAPTER ———— ———— THIRTEEN

'Sit down, Mr Hayward,' said Bragg, gesturing to the chair by Sir Walter's desk. 'I just want to clear up one or two matters.'

Hayward seemed less relaxed than when they had last seen him. There were dark smudges under his eyes, and his smile was perfunctory. Nevertheless, he arranged himself in the ·chair with dignity, carefully parting the tails of his morning coat to prevent their being creased, and crossing his legs elegantly.

'You said on Tuesday,' began Bragg, 'that at your long meeting with Sir Walter on the ninth you discussed the future management of the bank.'

'That is so,' replied Hayward.

'You told us that Sir Walter was considering withdrawing from the active management of the bank, because he had been told that he might be made a Minister of the Crown.'

Hayward acknowledged the statement with a nod.

'We asked the Prime Minister about this,' went on Bragg, 'and he said there was never the remotest possibility of Sir Walter being considered for high office.'

Hayward's jaw dropped with surprise, then he recovered. 'I don't know what the truth of the matter is,' he said with a deprecating smile. 'I can only tell you what Sir Walter said to me. Perhaps he deceived himself.'

Bragg looked stonily at Hayward for a long moment, then swung briskly round to a pile of documents on a side table.

'Will you take a look at this investment schedule please? . . . It was taken from the file of the Applin trust. Is it in your writing?'

Hayward placed his spectacles on his nose with a nervous hand. 'Yes, it is,' he said.

'You will see the last item is a row of leasehold houses in Rotherhithe Street. Did you cause this investment to be transferred in May out of the Compton Settlement into the Applin Settlement?'

Hayward's elegant bearing seemed to crumble. He looked out of the window at the stone fortress of the Bank of England, swallowed painfully, and turned back to Bragg. 'Yes, I did,' he said in a voice that was hardly audible.

'Constable Morton and I went to Rotherhithe Street after our meeting, and found that the houses were being torn down to make way for the new docks . . . Did you know that?'

'I . . . I . . .' muttered Hayward.

'Here is a letter of the fourteenth of May from White, Poppham and Crowley of Maidenhead, taken from the file of the Compton Settlement. In it Mr Crowley proposes an immediate valuation of the investments in the Settlement. Was it as a result of the letter that you transferred the houses to the Applin Settlement?'

Hayward was gazing at Bragg with unfocused eyes, as if mesmerized.

'On the same day, the twenty-first of May, shares in seven companies were also transferred from the Compton to the Applin Settlement. What was the consideration for the transfers?'

'Cash,' said Hayward in a hollow voice.

'And if we investigate the companies, shall we find they are as worthless as the property?'

Hayward took out a handkerchief and dabbed at the perspiration on his pallid face. 'I can see there is no point in concealment,' he said in a low voice, 'so I might as well make a clean breast of it.'

'Before you do, let me warn you that Constable Morton will take down everything you say in writing, and it may be used against you.'

'I understand . . . I suppose it was greed on my part,' began Hayward. 'It's the besetting sin of the new manager class. We are the people who keep the businesses going, but our contribution isn't recognized. The wealth we create goes to maintain the owner's family in idleness, and our plans can be scrapped by some ignoramus who just happens to have the right family connections.'

He passed his tongue over his lips. 'I joined the bank in Sir John Greville's time, and it was he who made me manager. He was an excessively prudent man, and it was due to him that the bank failed to take the commercial opportunities open to it. But at least, having stated his views, he allowed me to run the business accordingly. It was on my prompting that the business was turned into a company . . . my idea was to protect the trust funds if the bank failed. It seems ironic in retrospect, doesn't it? When Sir John died, Sir Walter became chairman, and immediately began to interfere in the running of the business. He knew little or nothing about it, but he insisted on having his way. He made several ill-advised investments, and it became apparent that if this course was adhered to, the bank would go under. Then, having virtually ruined the business, he became interested in politics and left me to rescue it . . . or rather I should say that his absence gave me the opportunity to try to rescue it.'

There was a pause as Hayward looked down at his carefully manicured hands. Then he took a deep breath, and went on in a firmer tone.

'You will be aware that I come from a relatively poor family. I have amassed a little capital during my working life, but not of a quantity that I considered either adequate or reasonable, having regard to my contribution to the bank. I am of such an age that I would find difficulty in obtaining a post commensurate with my experience and ability, should Wittrick and Greville fail. I endeavoured to provide for this contingency by applying to Sir Walter for an increase in my emolument, but he refused. Having crippled the bank by his wilful stupidity, he refused to pay me what I was worth on the grounds that business was poor. I am not trying to excuse what I've done. In a banker it can't be excused. I'm just trying to explain why I did it: what drove me to it. The idea came to me when one of the bank's debtors asked me for the renewal of a loan. It wasn't possible; the company was virtually insolvent, and the owner was too old to rebuild its fortunes. I told him I would have to call in the loan, but said I knew of someone who might be glad to be rid of it. I arranged for a nominee to buy the shares for twenty pounds, and then resold them to the Compton Settlement, which had sufficiently wide powers of investment, for five hundred pounds.'

'Was there no danger of your being detected?' asked Bragg.

'Very little. It was not apparent that I was behind the purchase and sale, and the other Compton trustee was inactive. Over the next two years I made six further purchases on the same principle, and sold the shares to the Compton Settlement.'

'And in each case the shares were virtually worthless?' asked Bragg.

'That is so.'

'Suppose Sir Walter had looked at the Compton file?'

'It was unlikely that he would do so, and if he did, I had arranged for an accountant to provide me with a supporting valuation.'

'I noticed there were no accounts of the business on the file,' remarked Bragg.

'We don't always ask for accounts . . . At one stage I considered persuading the accountant to provide me with bogus accounts, but I decided it would merely increase the risk that I would be found out.'

'And the properties?' asked Bragg.

'That was slightly different. I took them when the mortgagor defaulted. It was only later that I realized he had heard about the dock schemes, and decided he would leave the bank with the worthless property. Had I pursued him personally instead of giving him discharge against the property, I could have recovered the loan from his other assets.'

'So you transferred it from the bank's portfolio of investments to the Compton Settlement to cover up your mistake?'

'Yes.'

'When you got Mr Crowley's letter, you had no time to lose. Why did you choose the Applin Settlement to transfer these investments to?'

'I had little choice. We don't deal with many settlements

whose powers of investment would allow the purchase of shares in private companies. Nevertheless I didn't intend to leave them there for long. There was another Settlement I was going to pass them to, but we were just in the middle of the quinquennial valuation of the assets.'

'Another few weeks, and you'd have been safe?'

'Yes.' Hayward grimaced ruefully.

'Bad luck! What happened when Applin found out?'

'Sir Walter didn't say anything to me for a day or two. He must have been going through the files, and checking up on the companies. Then he called me in on the Thursday. I denied knowing anything about it, and said I had relied on one of the senior clerks who happened to be on holiday that week. I don't think Sir Walter believed me, but he couldn't prove anything one way or another till the clerk returned.'

'And what then?'

'I intended to pay the money back. Sir Walter wouldn't have prosecuted me, it would have been bad for the reputation of the bank.'

'Then why not confess on the Thursday?'

'I don't know. I hadn't thought it out clearly.'

'I know why,' said Bragg simply. 'You'd decided to murder him before his suspicions could be confirmed.'

Hayward's eyes opened in alarm. 'No! Not that! . . . I had nothing to do with his death . . . I didn't even know he'd been murdered . . .''

'Where were you on the evening of the tenth of July?'

'I was working late at the bank.'

'Anyone with you?'

'No, I was alone.'

'Covering up your peccadillos? All right. Arthur John Hayward, I have here a warrant for your arrest. You will be taken to Moor Lane police station, where you will be

charged with fraud. Other charges may be brought against
you later.'

When they called at the Belgravia home of Lady Gore,
Bragg and Morton found to their relief that the family was
away in the country. They were invited into the kitchen by a
rosy-faced young cook, with a fringe of fair hair escaping
from under her white cap.

'You and Mrs Roberts used to work for Sir Walter and
Lady Greville, didn't you?' asked Bragg.

'Yes, do you want to talk to Lily as well? She's about. I'll
fetch her if you like. Drink your tea, and I'll be back in two
shakes of a winkle's pin.' She bounced happily out of the
room.

'I'd say they'd done rather well for themselves,' observed Morton.

'Particularly when the family is away, eh? We're in the
wrong job lad . . . at least I am! You'd hardly envy the
servants of the aristocracy, when you're a nob yourself.'

'It's amusing really. At home they all seem so terribly
busy the whole time.'

'So did you, when you were on the beat and the sergeant
came round.'

Mrs Roberts was small, plump and bustling. She pointed-
ly refrained from sitting, but stood with her back to the
window, some kind of inventory in her hand.

'We were surprised to find that you had left the Grevilles'
employ so soon after Sir Walter's death,' observed Bragg.

'It wasn't us,' expostulated the cook. 'Her ladyship
wouldn't hear of us staying.'

'She was very nice with us,' interposed the housekeeper.
'She could have made us work out our notices, but she

wanted us particularly to take a place with her friend, Lady Gore.'

'I'm surprised Lady Gore was taking on staff at this time of year,' said Morton.

Mrs Roberts looked him up and down with distaste. 'If you came from a better background,' she replied severely, 'you would know that the best domestic servants have to be engaged when they are available.'

Bragg's eyes gleamed with amusement at Morton's discomfiture. 'Was Lady Greville a good employer?' he asked.

'Yes, very good,' asserted Mrs Roberts. 'She had her little ways, but then they all have.'

'What little ways?'

'She insisted that people did their job properly, but that's right. It's what they get paid for. I had no quarrel with that.'

'She'd sometimes change her mind on the spur of the moment,' remarked the cook. 'She'd settle the menu for a dinner party, then she might hear that afternoon there was asparagus or some such in the shops, and she'd be sending Tom to Leadenhall market or Spitalfields for some. She'd not rest till she got some.'

'I gather that you had to prepare a buffet each month for the committee meeting. Who decided what to buy?' asked Bragg.

'Her ladyship. She arranged for all the food. I just prepared it.'

'Was there anything special that night?'

'Not that I can remember.'

'What about drink?' asked Bragg. 'Did they usually drink heavily?'

'No,' replied Mrs Roberts. 'I could tell from the decanters, and they drank very little really. The meetings were early in the evening, you see.'

'What about that last meeting?'

'The weather was so warm that Sir Walter rang down for some beer. I took up a dozen bottles, and there were four left in the morning.'

'And the decanters?'

'They were hardly down at all.'

'So you saw the men at the meeting?'

'Yes, I knew them all well. They'd been coming to the house regularly for years.'

'Were they personal friends, or did they only go to the house for Tory Party functions?'

'The latter, really.' Mrs Roberts pursed her lips together disapprovingly. 'Mr Winterslow did come to the house one afternoon when Sir Walter was at the bank . . . and her ladyship received him . . . alone.'

'I expect it was all perfectly innocent,' smiled Bragg. 'When was that?'

'Just after they'd got back from Fulford. I'd say the first of July.'

'Did he stay long?'

'Too long for her own good,' replied the housekeeper censoriously.

'What about the night of Sir Walter's death?' asked Bragg.

Mrs Roberts hesitated. 'I said to cook, didn't I, Alice? I thought I saw Major Applin that same night. I took the dog for a walk late on.'

'How late?'

'Round about eleven I suppose. I wasn't much bothered about the time. But I thought I saw the major walking up Circus Place towards the house.'

'Are you saying you walked through the hall at eleven o'clock and everything was normal?' asked Bragg with a show of excitement.

'No, I came up the area steps at the far end of the house, away from the entrance. And I walked clockwise round the Circus, so I was on the opposite side when I saw the major. That's why I can't be certain.'

'I see. And what was the relationship like between Sir Walter and his wife? Were they on good terms?'

The two women looked at each other, and Alice giggled.

'Like most married couples,' said Mrs Roberts, 'they would quarrel from time to time.'

'You could hear them downstairs if the baize door was open,' chimed in Alice.

'What did they quarrel about?' asked Bragg with an amused smile.

'Money, mostly,' replied the housekeeper.

'Who would get the better of it?'

'Her ladyship generally. She had a sharp tongue when the fit was on her.'

'Did they quarrel on the day Sir Walter died?' asked Bragg.

'Not that day. But they had a real up-and-downer after dinner the night before.'

'What were they fighting about?'

'I'm not sure. Money came into it. Her ladyship was going on about not having enough, and something about using her money for the benefit of the Tories. Then he shouted something about Switzerland, and she banged out of the house.'

'Well, thank you, ladies. You've been very helpful. And thank you for the tea.'

'It must be very annoying,' observed Bragg as they walked away, 'not being able to have a real ding-dong without the servants overhearing you.'

'I'd never realized how much they must know about

one,' said Morton apologetically. 'One tends to ignore them.'

'Believe me, lad, you get to know more through talking to the servants than through questioning their masters . . . I'll tell you one thing. It's time we sent a cable to the Swiss police to find out what's known of our friend Roquebrun.'

Catherine Marsden had been excited to receive a summons from the editor. She even took five minutes to tidy her hair and smooth her dress. When she arrived in his cluttered office, however, it seemed unlikely that he would be hanging triumphal garlands round her neck. He was staring moodily at a sheet of paper which Catherine recognized as her copy for the next edition. She smiled sweetly at him, and thought she detected a softening in his demeanour.

'I don't know, Miss Marsden,' he said with a sigh. 'This is a bit beyond our normal coverage. We aren't *The Times* you know. Are you sure this is all solid fact?'

'Yes, Mr Tranter, I've been careful to make clear any areas of speculation.'

'I would prefer there to be no speculation whatsoever.'

'But then it wouldn't be an article, it would just be a recital of facts,' objected Catherine.

'That's what the *City Press* has always been, a catalogue of the happenings in London, an urbane record of the changing face of the City, an informed commentary on the commercial and social scene in the trading capital of the world. We don't see ourselves as in competition with the dailies.'

'But surely if there is a matter of genuine interest happening within the City, we have as much of a duty to bring it to the notice of the public as *The Times* or the *Star*?'

'I don't know.' Tranter sighed unhappily. 'Not everybody was pleased about your piece in Wednesday's edition. I've had a number of letters this morning, complaining about it, saying that it's our duty to support the police, and talking about the war against crime.'

Catherine summoned up what she hoped was a winsome smile. 'But there were some letters that supported it?' she asked.

'Oh yes. I have to admit that . . . but not so many as took me to task over it.'

'I suppose it was the men who condemned the article and the women who applauded it?' remarked Catherine.

'Yes . . . that's broadly true,' replied Tranter, glancing at a pile of letters on his desk.

'Then that's good,' exclaimed Catherine triumphantly. 'We are achieving what we set out to do.'

'I'm not sure that we were right. I've always seen us as complementary to the dailies. We can't deal with national and international news, as they can, and I don't think we should try. We have a very special niche in journalism, covering the operation of the economic forces that really shape the world's destiny. I've no desire to become just another newspaper.'

'You make it sound like an even duller version of the *Economist*,' said Catherine lightly, 'and it isn't at all. It's a very civilized and cultured newspaper, and we are trying to get women to realize this. They may not be very interested in what is going on in China or Argentina, but they are interested in what's happening in their immediate surroundings. And they feel passionately about injustice and poverty.'

Tranter held up his hands, half smiling. 'I know all that, and we agreed it should be your area of concern. But we have to set sensible limits. After all, it's the men who buy our paper, not their wives. We want to achieve a situation where more men buy a copy because they know their wives will want to read it. The inescapable commercial fact is that we can't afford to alienate the men, in an effort to titillate the social consciences of their womenfolk . . . Now with regard to this piece, I want you to rewrite it, cutting out most of the speculation, and particularly this bit at the end hitting at corruption in high places. After all,' he smiled, 'although we may be parochial, you have the advantage of writing for a highly-informed and intelligent readership. You don't need to waste time stating the obvious.'

'Very well,' replied Catherine with relief, 'I'll let you have it this afternoon.'

'And why don't you send a note round to Lady Greville. See if you can get her reaction to the rumours. There's something that would interest the fair sex.'

CHAPTER ——— ——— FOURTEEN

After fruitless visits to Coopers Row and Billingsgate Market, Bragg and Morton found Winterslow at the Fishmongers' Hall. They waited amid its classical splendour until the committee meeting ended, and Winterslow conducted them to a small room overlooking the Thames.

'How are you getting on, sergeant?' he asked cheerfully. 'Made any arrests yet?'

'Just the one, sir,' replied Bragg.

'Excellent. Who is he?'

'The public will have to wait just a little longer, sir. Now I want to go back to the committee meeting again. We know that what you have told us is not right. It wasn't the bland correct affair you made it out to be. In fact Sir Walter was fighting for his political life. In an odd way the business advances he had made in order to secure support originally, all seemed to have been disastrous; except, that is, for the

147

loans to your company. If we take Mr Plowright as an example, he had funded his inventions far beyond the limit that commercial prudence dictated. When he had to terminate that support, he turned Plowright from a possible opponent into an avowed enemy. The same process seems to have been occurring with other people, though it hadn't gone quite as far. When he received the agenda with ''Parlimentary representation'' on it, however, he must have realized that the subtle influence of obligation would not serve him anymore; and he decided he would have to use naked threats or inducements if he were to beat off the challenge. As a result he arranged to meet most of the key figures on the committee in the week prior to the meeting. He saw you on the seventh of July. I want you to tell me what really went on at that meeting.'

'In a way I was forewarned,' said Winterslow reflectively. 'Since I would have succeeded Sir Walter, had he been deposed, I tended to hear snippets of news and gossip from all his opponents. The weekend before the committee meeting, I was told by Luke Plowright that Sir Walter had offered to resume the financing of his moving-picture projector.'

'When did this happen?' asked Bragg.

'The Friday before.'

'And what was Mr Plowright's reaction?'

'Mixed. He was very bitter that he had been let down earlier. He could see that it was a blatant attempt to buy his vote. He talked wildly about Greville not being fit to live on the same planet . . . that was just his way. I'm sure he wouldn't have taken any physical action against Sir Walter. At the same time Plowright was penniless, his self-respect destroyed. I think he was tempted by the offer. Five thousand pounds would have set him up again. I gather Sir Walter had indicated clearly that the bank wouldn't look too closely into the way the money was spent, and would be prepared to write it off after a year.'

'That's corruption on a grand scale,' remarked Bragg. 'Did Plowright accept?'

'He neither accepted nor rejected the offer. He just said that he would think about it. He then went to see his wife and her parents, to get their views on what he should do. They are rather proper, religious people, and they weren't very helpful. He saw me the night before the committee meeting. He was still in a quandary, the more so because he felt his vote could decide the matter one way or the other.'

'How did he see the votes falling?' asked Bragg.

'Oh, Bridson, Applin, me and Plowright in favour of a change; Wheeler—that's the other MP—Greville and Kimber against.'

'So it only needed Plowright to change sides for Sir Walter to be safe?'

'That's how he saw it.'

'Why was he sure Applin would vote against Sir Walter?' asked Morton.

'That's something you'll have to ask him.'

'But, of course, Sir Walter had put similar pressure on you in the meantime,' said Bragg.

'Yes. It was a very crude threat. Either I pledged my support or he would call in the loan his bank had made to my company.'

'Which would mean you would have lost not only your business, but your residence also.'

Winterslow's eyes narrowed momentarily. 'I see you know all about it. Yes, I was put in a difficult position. The business couldn't hope to find the money to repay the loan, so I bought time by saying that I would not vote against him. I immediately set about trying to find an alternative source of funds, but it wasn't possible before the meeting.'

'So Plowright had a financial interest in seeing that Sir Walter stayed alive,' remarked Bragg conversationally, 'whereas you would have been better off with him dead.'

Winterslow laughed uneasily. 'On the contrary. Every banker I've approached to refinance my company seems to know that I am likely to be Sir Walter's successor. So far they have turned me down to a man, on the grounds that without my own continuous involvement, the business will not generate enough profit to justify the loan.'

'Except that Wittrick and Greville aren't likely to call it in now.'

'There is that, I suppose.'

'What happened at the meeting, then?'

'There was a general discussion, mainly between Bridson the chairman and Kimber the treasurer, about the reasons for the disenchantment with Greville. Both put the case of their respective sides. Then, as I'd agreed with Plowright the night before, I moved "next business". Since I was the potential successor, Bridson played to my lead, and the motion was carried.'

'So Sir Walter had won?' asked Bragg.

'Not really. It would be nearer the truth to say we hadn't lost. We could easily bring up the matter again when I was out of Greville's clutches.'

'But that would hardly clinch matters. I thought it was Plowright's vote that was the key to it.'

Winterslow flushed. 'I'd said I would try to find him a job with my company . . . But he would have had to work. You may be sure of that.'

'I see,' said Bragg drily. 'Now you went to see Lady Greville on the first of July. What was that about?'

Winterslow looked puzzled for a moment. 'Ah, I remember now,' he said. 'I'm on the committee of the Holborn Union. Lady Greville was organizing a charity function for the inmates of the workhouse there. Nothing sinister, sergeant, I assure you!'

'You sent for me, sergeant.' Applin looked about Bragg's room with interest, taking in the bare windows, the scuffed desk and cracked linoleum. His face for once was almost animated.

'Sit down, will you, sir,' said Bragg, pausing to light his pipe. Morton realized that Bragg's pipe was an infallible indicator of the tone an interview would take. This friendly puffing, with a contented look on his face, meant a relaxed, even flippant approach. If Bragg began to scrape the bowl of his pipe, or even took it to pieces and cleaned it, there was an implication that he was floundering. At such times his face took on a mournful look, inviting confidences, relaxing vigilance. The ragged moustache had been an essential part of this pose, which would not be so effective now it had been trimmed, for the mouth below was anything but irresolute. Morton smiled to himself at the thought that the discharge of public business could be affected because of a few words on a square of pasteboard.

'You know,' went on Bragg, 'if there were such an offence as misleading the police in their enquiries, I'd lock you up here and now. You've done nothing but fob us off with half-truths every time we've seen you. Last time, you said that at your meeting with Sir Walter on the sixth you'd had nothing more than an inconclusive chat with him about some changes in investments. We checked up on the new investments and found they were all worthless. The Rotherhithe Street houses, for instance, were just rubble, to make away for the Surrey Docks. Now you can't tell me you didn't know that.'

Applin twisted the ends of his moustache, a gleam of amusement in his eyes.

'I should tell you,' continued Bragg, 'that Mr Hayward, the manager, and lately the director of the bank, has confessed that these investments were made by him in the course of a scheme to defraud the clients of the bank. He has now been arrested.'

'Hayward's in prison?' asked Applin, with a vindictive smile.

'He's out on bail now. We shall be needing you to give evidence . . . we're a bit short of other witnesses!' Bragg chuckled. 'Probably be next month at the Guildhall. And so that we know what you're going to say, perhaps you'll tell us what happened at that last meeting with Sir Walter . . . but mind it's the truth, now.'

'I admit that I knew about the investments.' Applin smiled disarmingly. 'Or all but two of the companies. Like you, I suppose, I took a cab to Rotherhithe Street. When I saw Greville, I challenged him. He wouldn't lie to me about a thing like that. Anyway, he sent for the trust file and we examined it, but it was no more informative than my own papers . . . You don't think he was in it with Hayward, do you?'

'Our enquiries are only just beginning on that aspect,' replied Bragg non-committally.

'Anyway, I wasn't inclined to suspend judgment till Greville had spoken to Hayward. After all, I'd seen the flattened properties for myself. So I became very angry, and threatened to sue the bank for breach of trust.' He paused, and gazed out of the window reflectively. 'It seems that we may all have underestimated Sir Walter's ability, because if he really knew nothing of Hayward's fraud, then he turned the situation to his advantage with remarkable skill.'

'In what way, sir?'

'I've said already that I won't discuss the private transactions of the constituency committee.'

'You needn't worry about that, sir,' observed Bragg cheerfully. 'Mr Winterslow has told us all about the split, and Sir Walter's efforts to keep his seat. I shall be asking you how he tried to influence your vote.'

'I see,' Applin hesitated for a moment. 'In that case I have no reason for reticence. As I said, I threatened to sue the bank, and in riposte he produced the Deed of Settlement. This has the most extraordinary indemnity clause one could ever imagine. It seems to protect the bank and its officers from any kind of proceedings, even if they had been deliberately fraudulent. I was somewhat taken aback, as you can imagine. I have very little personal capital, and the trust monies were in the control of the bank I proposed to sue. I suppose I might have brought an action to have them removed as trustees, but that wouldn't necessarily alter the past. Anyway, Greville protested that he would endeavour to make good any loss the trust might have suffered. He said that if I took proceedings against the bank they would have to be resisted, and I would lose. Nevertheless, if I refrained from proceedings he would make an *ex gratia* payment into the trust to put things right. He made it sound that the payment would come from his personal fortune. There was one condition: I was to support him at the coming committee meeting.'

'And did you?' asked Bragg.

'As you must know, it didn't come to a vote.'

'You said you went to Sir Walter's funeral,' remarked Bragg after a pause.

'That's right.'

'Where was it?'

'At Fulford Hall, near St Albans.'

'In the village church?'

'No. The service was held in the chapel, and then we went down to the mausoleum in the private graveyard.' Applin smiled sardonically. 'Very impressive it was, the coffin on the shoulders of six farm workers, all with new suits for the occasion, and half the City of London pacing solemnly behind.'

'You seem to get a certain amount of amusement out of it.'

'Not at the time. I was as affected as anyone by the occasion. But in retrospect I can't forbear a wry smile at the incongruity between the public grief and the character of the man as I knew him.'

'You were actually in the mausoleum?'

'Yes, with the Bishop of London, the Lord Mayor, the Sheriffs, the other MP and the committee members . . . and of course the widow.'

Bragg knocked out his pipe, and placed it in the glass ash-tray. When he spoke again his voice was brisk and hard.

'Sir Walter Greville was murdered. We know that now. And in looking for his murderer we are very interested in anyone who has lied consistently to us during our en-quiries.'

'But I'm not lying to you now,' protested Applin.

'Then again, you came to the conclusion that we were going to have a belated post-mortem examination done on the body . . . When we got there we found the head was missing.'

'Really?' exclaimed Applin with a tinge of excitement in his husky voice.

'You knew where the corpse was, and could have taken away the head.'

'When was this?' asked Applin.

'Wednesday night.'

'I see,' said Applin with a glint of triumph in his eyes.

'Well, I'm sorry that I can't help you, sergeant. I'm afraid I did not behead Sir Walter, though I admit I would have relished the idea a fortnight ago.'

'Then, of course, you were seen on the night of the murder, going back to the Grevilles' house.'

'Who says I went back?' asked Applin, a frown creasing his forehead.

'The housekeeper, Mrs Roberts. She says she knows you well.'

'Apparently not well enough, sergeant. I deny that I went back to the house that night, just as I deny having taken off Greville's head. If I misled you at our earlier meetings it was in an attempt to protect other people.'

'From what?' asked Bragg brusquely.

'Police enquiries can do irreparable damage even to the innocent.'

'More like you were protecting yourself.'

'Sergeant, it must be clear to you that I had nothing to gain from Greville's death. While he lived I had the expectation that the speculations of Hayward would be made good. Now that he is dead, the possibility seems remote.'

'Money isn't the only thing that matters,' said Bragg. 'It isn't even the chief thing. I think you killed him in a rage. It wouldn't be the first time, would it?'

Applin ignored the innuendo. 'Is it not correct,' he asked, 'that your enquiries were set on foot by the coroner because he received a card with the message "Our Honourable Member. Was it really an accident?" on it? I sent that card.'

A silence fell in the room, and Morton could feel the tension which Bragg had created slowly draining away. They were back to the comfortable atmosphere of the beginning, and none of them seemed inclined to break it.

Then Bragg picked up his pipe. 'All right,' he said

gruffly, 'you can go. But don't go far. If you try to leave London I'll have you in chokey before you've set off.'

The major stood up, carefully settled the tails of his morning coat, then, smiling secretly to himself, strode out of the room.

'That bastard is always just one jump ahead of us,' exclaimed Bragg crossly.

'The thing that struck me as odd,' replied Morton, 'is that when you said Sir Walter was murdered, he didn't seem at all surprised.'

'I wonder if I've done the right thing. It was the coroner's card bit that decided me to let him go. I swear no one but us, Primrose and the Commissioner knew about that. But he might have heard a whisper and be bluffing us.'

'He did get the words exactly right, though.'

'But why send it in the first place? If he had suspicions, why not come out with it? Did you notice how excited he was, particularly over the head . . . I've seen this sort of reaction before. The criminal realizes we're on to him, and has to try to throw us off the scent. He becomes involved in a kind of ritual with us, almost detached from the outcome; like playing out a game of chess when you've only got a knight and bishop left. If I'm right, he's unlikely to do a bunk, but by the same token he won't make it easy for us. I think, come Monday, we'll get a search warrant and see what we can find.'

CHAPTER _____
_____ FIFTEEN

Morton strode breezily into Bragg's room next morning to find the sergeant in shirt sleeves, gloomily pulling at his moustache.

'There are so many people in this case with good reason to want Greville dead, and so many of them with the opportunity to murder him that it should be easy. And yet I can't seem to build a solid case against any of them. With every one there's something missing.'

'In that case, we're unlikely to arrest anyone today, so can I play cricket for Blackheath this afternoon?'

'Cricket! . . . Well, if you must; so long as we can finish at the bank.'

'Splendid! Thank you. Anything new this morning?'

'The post-mortem report from Dr Burney. It doesn't help.' Bragg tossed a couple of typewritten foolscap sheets to Morton. 'If you boil it down, all it says is that there was nothing in the bits of Sir Walter available for examination that could have caused his death. We've been working on that basis for days.'

'At least it confirms your hypothesis. It also justifies our favourite newspaper. Miss Catherine Marsden is really spreading her wings in the *City Press* this morning. I can't help feeling that when you virtually challenged her to get the information herself, you merely put her on her mettle.'

'What does it say?' asked Bragg sourly.

'It starts by mentioning the rumours circulating in the City concerning the death of Sir Walter Greville. Then it gives a not very flattering account of the coroner's inquest, and reports that when their correspondent called to see the coroner, he was not at home.'

'Typical nasty bit of innuendo.'

'That's not all. She goes on to report a conversation with a Major George Applin, who claimed to be a close acquaintance of the deceased. He asserted that the police were enquiring into the circumstances of Sir Walter's death, and said he had it on the highest authority that they were going to exhume his body.'

'My God! What's he playing at?'

'Perhaps he's reinforcing the bluff.'

'Come on, lad, let's get out of here before the Commissioner sends for us.'

The morning was cloudless, with a light cooling breeze from the east. Morton felt elated at the prospect of playing cricket on the tree-fringed ground at Blackheath, so much like Tonbridge or Maidstone. He could anticipate the tingle in his hands from a hard slip catch, hear the polite applause from the deck-chairs which acknowledged a stylish boundary. No doubt the Blackheath Club would expect fireworks from him; well, he wouldn't disappoint them.

They were greeted at the bank by the chief clerk.

'Who's in charge now?' asked Bragg.

'I am,' he grinned.

'Promotion's rapid here! Who's next in line, when we take you in?'

'Nobody. I've sacked everybody else!'

'What's going to happen to the bank?'

'I don't know. It's terrible really. We weren't what you call busy at the best of times, but now it's like a morgue. Not that there's anyone here to take a decision if a customer did come in . . . It's my idea they'll sell the business; it'll never get over all this trouble.'

'Would you mind that?'

'So long as I kept my job, I wouldn't care who owned it.'

Morton's heart sank when he unlocked the cupboard in Sir Walter's room and saw the stack of files and ledgers within. However, most of the files related to Lady Greville's first marriage settlement, many of the papers pre-dating her marriage to Sir Walter. After half an hour they had set aside a small pile of account books and papers which needed to be examined. Bragg tossed a slim ledger at him.

'That's the cash book in which the transactions of the marriage settlement are recorded. What I'm interested in is the amount of money they spent in, say, twelve months to the thirtieth of June this year. Sir Walter seems to have made a note by every entry showing what it was for, or where it came from, so it shouldn't be difficult. I'll look through Sir Walter's own bank account.'

They settled companionably on each side of the desk, and began to examine the ledgers, making notes as they went.

'I've got an entry here marked "Xfer",' said Morton. 'I suppose that means "Transfer". The question is: where to?'

'What date was it?' asked Bragg.

'Two hundred pounds on September the third last year.'

Bragg turned back a page in his ledger. 'Yes, here it is . . . Let's both list all the transfers, and we'll compare them later.'

In half an hour Morton had finished, and sat back with growing impatience as Bragg meticulously made additions to his long column of figures. He wondered what was the latest train which would get him to Blackheath by two o'clock. He realized he didn't know whether he would have to catch it at London Bridge or Charing Cross. Now Bragg was totalling his sheet, whispering the numbers to himself as he went. Then he threw down his pencil, and took up his pipe.

'Well, I make it that Sir Walter spent just over twelve thousand pounds on living expenses in the last twelve months. And don't forget that the running expenses of the Hertfordshire house are met by the trust. Do you think that's enough for them to live on?'

'It seems a great deal of money, particularly as Lady Greville's personal expenses, such as dressmaker and florist, are paid from her marriage settlement.'

'I can't find a reference to any other accounts in Sir Walter's name,' said Bragg. 'And you can see where his salary from the bank comes in each month, and where the income from the family trust is credited each March. Now where is your list of transfers?'

Morton passed over his sheet of paper. 'You might have totalled them,' remarked Bragg irritably. 'No matter, I can see they are the same as the credits to this account. So this is the position: Sir Walter's own income was around seven thousand pounds, their expenses were twelve thousand, and the difference was made up by transfers from Lady Greville's marriage settlement. Interesting isn't it? You

remember the cook? She said they had a real ding-dong the
night before Sir Walter was murdered; about him using her
money. And Switzerland came into it as well. I think we'll
just pop round to Finsbury Circus and have a word with
her . . . Don't worry, lad, it won't take a minute.'

They were left standing in the hall by Mrs Shorter, as
usual, but this time Lady Greville came down to see them.
She was pale and clearly upset.

'Oh, sergeant, have you seen the dreadful things they are
saying in the paper this morning?' she cried.

'You shouldn't take too much notice of that ma'am,'
replied Bragg. 'Newspaper folk are a scurrilous lot.'

'But to talk of exhumation, it's indecent . . . and poor
Dr Primrose. He was the kindest man in the world.'

'You mustn't let yourself be upset by these people,' said
Bragg in a fatherly way. 'Your husband was a public figure,
and he would understand that the papers would be interested
in him to the very end.'

'But surely it isn't true?'

'It doesn't matter whether it's true or not. Life's got to go
on for you after it's all over. Why don't you go away for a
bit?'

'Perhaps I should. I wanted to be here in case you needed
me.'

'Just let us know where you are, so that we can contact
you when we need to.'

'Thank you, sergeant. I might well follow your advice.'

'You can clear up one point of difficulty now, if you
would. We've been looking at your husband's financial
records for the past twelve months, and we find that the total
living expenses were around twelve thousand pounds, while
his income was only a little over seven thousand pounds.
Have you any idea where he got the other five thousand
from?'

'Of course, sergeant. It came from the income in my marriage settlement, of which the bank was trustee.'

'And you were aware of that, and in agreement with it?' asked Bragg.

'Naturally. He was, after all, my husband.'

Bragg sighed as they regained the street. 'I can't quite make her out,' he said. 'What she says doesn't quite chime with what she does; like dismissing her servants and still living on in that house.'

'Does everyone have to act with absolute logic all the time?' asked Morton.

'No, you're right. It's just an uneasy feeling I have about her. Probably it's because I've never mixed with society women. What do you think of her?'

'After your strictures the other day, I'm afraid of giving any opinion on women,' laughed Morton. 'If I tried very hard to be objective, I would say that she must be fairly robust, because she got over her first husband's death, even though she was distraught for months. She must be well organized, because she carries off the part of a political hostess with consummate ease; and that can't be easy. She seems to be determined, but fair, if her servants are to be believed. Beyond that, my objectivity succumbs, because I find her enormously attractive and charming.'

'Well lad, you've described the lady she wants the world to see. I'd give a lot to have been the chamber maid, and listened to them quarrelling. Ah well, I suppose we ought to pop into the office to see what's doing. Then we'll call it a day."

They sneaked up the stairs, fearful of a summons from the Commissioner, and gained Bragg's office. A yellow envelope lay on the desk. Bragg tore it open, and looked at the contents in perplexity. 'It's a telegram from Geneva, in French. Here you are, lad, what's it say?'

Morton read it through quickly. 'It's in reply to our cable about Roquebrun. The Geneva police know him well. He once was one of their officers. It seems he now does private investigations for persons in the Geneva area.'

'And he came to see Sir Walter, after some correspondence between them.' Bragg gazed at Morton for a moment, then made a grimace. 'I'm sorry, lad, but there's precious little use in my going. And I shall want you back here by Monday morning. I'll tell you what, next time you're playing cricket I'll come and watch you myself. Just to show there's no ill feelings.'

Morton arrived in Geneva at seven o'clock, and since it was Sunday morning the city was deserted. The sun was rising over the distant mountains, and the air was fresh and cool. He strolled past offices and shops, all seeming to cater for the wealthy; furs in July, jewellery, watches and more watches. Then he could see the lake, framed as through a window by the tall stone buildings and the branches of the trees bordering the street. He walked down to a pier jutting into the lake, and stretched out on a bench in the sun. He had spent the evening by the rail of the ferry boat, watching the sun sinking blood-red behind thin streamers of cloud, then dropping quickly, like a capsized ship, into the sea. For the rest of the night he had tried to sleep, propped up in the corner of a train compartment. Now his muscles were as tired as if he'd run ten miles, and his joints felt rusty. He turned on his side, and consciously relaxed his body. He was just drifting into a light doze when church bells began to peal nearby. He sat up and looked at his watch. A quarter to eight. If he turned up at half past nine it should be about right. He rubbed his bristly chin; he'd better get tidied up, or he'd stand little chance of getting information from anyone. He wandered down the pier to where some sailors were scrubbing down the deck of an excursion steamer, and they directed him to a hotel nearby.

An hour later, having been shaved, with his clothes brushed, and having breakfasted, he set off with a jaunty air to find Roquebrun. Quai de l'Ile was on the edge of the shopping centre of Geneva. At first sight number fifty-one did not exist, the numbers jumping from forty-seven on one block to fifty-three on the next. Morton retraced his steps and found a narrow arcade between them. It was bordered on each side with mean stalls, some with rough shutters to protect their wares, others little more than a table against the wall. The flag floor was worn and uneven; what light there was came through a grimy glass roof. Half way down the arcade was a flight of wooden steps leading upwards. He looked for a number, or a name-plate but there was none. Still, this seemed to be the only possibility. He climbed to the first landing. Here there were two offices, one apparently occupied by an accountant, the other by an exporting company. On the next floor the offices merely bore name-plates, without any indication of the nature of the activities carried on within. From the corner of the landing a narrower flight of stairs ran upwards. On the wall above them was painted 'Privée'. Morton hesitated, then went up. At the top was a small landing lit only by the light filtering through the opaque glass of a single door. There was neither number, name, nor bell. He rapped briskly on the door, and half-turned away. Nothing happened. He hammered at the door again, and placed his ear to the glass. So much for his vision of a buxom welcoming wife and chubby children. Then he thought he heard a door close within. He knocked and rattled the door again.

'Who is there?' called a man's voice.

'I wish to speak with M. Roquebrun.'

'Who are you?'

'I am police, from London.'

There was the rattle of a chain, and the door was opened by a middle-aged man, unshaven, and with tousled grey hair. A worn dressing-gown was thrown over his nightshirt, and his feet were bare.

'What do you want?' he asked.

'Are you R. Roquebrun?'

'Yes, that's right.'

'I've come to talk to you about one of your clients. I apologize if it is inconvenient.'

'No matter, come in.' Roquebrun showed him into a dingy living room, the remains of a meal still on the table from the night before, the chairs littered with books and papers.

'I am sorry if it is a little untidy. I do not get many visitors . . . Now what is it you wish to see me about?'

Morton cleared the litter from an armchair and sat down in a friendly and relaxed attitude. 'You went to London on the eighth of this month?'

Roquebrun did not appear to have heard the question.

'When you were there,' went on Morton, 'you had a meeting with Sir Walter Greville of Wittrick and Greville, the bankers in Lothbury. You had previously corresponded with him. Is that correct?'

'It is possible.'

'Two days after your visit, Sir Walter was murdered; we think there may be a link between them.'

'Why should this be?' asked Roquebrun.

'He was a banker. We think he may have been involved with international financial operations, or have been pursuing a foreign debtor we know nothing about. Our enquiries in London have revealed no obvious reason for murder, so we are widening our investigation.'

'You honour me, if you are suggesting that I would be employed in a matter of high finance,' said Roquebrun with a half smile. 'My concerns are normally with runaway minors and erring spouses.'

'Nevertheless it is important that we should know why Sir Walter consulted you, what instructions he gave you and what you discovered.'

'And if I refuse?'

'I am instructed to go to the Commissioner of Police for the canton, and obtain his assistance.'

Roquebrun fished a half-smoked cigarette from the pocket of his dressing-gown, and lit it. Then he smiled cynically. 'When your belly is empty, you cannot afford high-minded ethics.'

'When were you first approached by Sir Walter?' asked Morton.

Roquebrun crossed to a bookcase, and took a pile of folders from the bottom shelf. 'I am afraid you will be disappointed,' he said. 'I think it was merely an affair mafrimonial . . . Ah, here we are. I received a letter from Sir Walter on the twenty-fifth of May, asking if I would undertake a commission for him. He specified that my reply should be addressed to him at the bank and marked "Personal and Confidential". I see that I wrote in acceptance on the twenty-seventh.'

'And after that?'

'On the first of June, my client wrote to me giving his instructions. He said that in March and April of eighteen-ninety his wife had spent an extended holiday in Switzerland. She stayed at the Hôtel du Lac, here in Geneva. He wished to know what she had done, and whom she had seen.'

'Not very easy, so long after the event,' remarked Morton.

'Ah, but I still have my good friends in the police force, and we Swiss are more discriminating about our visitors than you are. We like to keep a discreet eye on them.'

'So what happened?'

'On the eleventh of June I wrote, as instructed, saying that I was ready to present my report, and I received an immediate reply, ordering me to attend at the bank on the afternoon of the eighth of July. I remember that I was very surprised that he should not be more anxious to have my report.'

'He always spends the last two weeks of June in the country, and I suppose he would not have wished you to be seen there. So on the eighth you made your report?'

'Yes. I was able to tell him that almost as soon as his wife arrived at the hotel she was taken ill, and spent the majority of her holiday at l'Hôpital Beauregard.'

'Didn't he know that?'

'It would appear that he did not. He told me that he had continued to receive letters on Hôtel du Lac notepaper, and had sent his replies there.'

'Was he surprised?'

'I think not. It seemed that I had confirmed a suspicion, perhaps a rumour he had heard. One often finds this in matrimonial enquiries.'

'What kind of hospital is it?'

'It is in two parts. The main building is a sanatorium for tuberculosis which is very successful, and well-known throughout Europe. There is, however, a clinic and nursing-home in the grounds which is owned by some French doctors. What goes on there is kept very discreet, but one can make guesses . . .' Roquebrun winked knowingly.

'I'm sorry, I must be very stupid. What do you think?'

'Well, France is a Catholic country. Measures against pregnancy are forbidden. But often a woman does not carry a child for more than a few weeks . . . especially if her doctor is compliant.'

'An abortion! Did Sir Walter ask you to verify that?'

'No. He was satisfied with my report, and paid my fee on the spot.'

'And you haven't found out anything since?'

'M'sieur, investigations are my business, not my hobby.'

'Where is the hospital?'

'Three kilometres away on the road to St Julien.'

'Thank you.' Morton shook Roquebrun's hand. 'You've been very helpful. I'm grateful.'

Morton took a cab to the hospital, and, instructing the driver to wait for him, walked up the imposing driveway. It led to a large infirmary with balconies on each storey. The windows were wide open, and through the wrought-iron railings he could see chair-beds lined up in the sun. To his left a narrower drive curved away to a clump of trees lower down the hill. As the branches swayed in the breeze, he could see the blue slate of a roof. Following the drive he found himself in front of a low modern building. It was formed of two wings at right angles, and the space between them was filled with a paved terrace and rockery gardens. Five or six women were sitting in deck-chairs, sheltered from the wind. None of them seemed over thirty-five. Morton strolled across the terrace to the entrance-hall, and rang the bell on the reception desk. In response a rather flustered young woman in nurse's uniform hurried in from a back room.

'I'm sorry,' she said. 'I was helping Veronique with the flowers.'

'Please don't worry,' said Morton with a smile. 'My name is Sir Walter Greville. You are expecting me.'

A startled look crossed the girl's face. 'No, I am sorry, we are expecting no one today.'

'But surely you got my letter? You must have done. I wrote to you over a week ago.'

'I have not been told that any visitor was expected today.'

'I'm not a visitor. I wanted to consult the doctor who cared for my wife when she was here last year.'

'Which doctor was it?'

'I can't remember. She gave me the name, but once I had written to you I threw the piece of paper away.'

'Perhaps if I look in her records I shall be able to discover it.'

She crossed to a cupboard, and unlocking it began to check through the files.'

'What was her full name?' she asked.

'Lady Beatrice Greville.'

'Yes, here is her file.'

She brought the folder over to her table and opened it. A white sheet of paper was stuck inside the front cover, which appeared to contain a summary of the case.

'Her doctor was M. Alibert. I'm afraid he is in Paris. He only comes here when he has a patient.'

'I suppose my letter has been sent on to him. How irritating!' Morton frowned bad-temperedly, and the girl began to look anxious. Then he smiled. 'But I'm sure you can help me. It's just that we want to have a child now, and don't seem to be able to. I wanted to find out discreetly from Dr Alibert whether there is any reason why my wife should not be able to conceive. I would think that if there were, he might have made a reference to it in his clinical notes.'

The girl looked dubiously at him, then began quickly to scan the papers. 'There's a reference to complications here, severe bleeding that took several days to respond to treatment . . . but that was when she lost her first baby.' She flicked over some more pages. 'It presumably took five years before she became pregnant again, so there must have been some after-effects. But she did become pregnant, so there can have been no permanent damage. Certainly, when she lost her baby last year, everything was perfectly normal.'

Morton's return journey was uneventful, and he was back in London shortly after eleven o'clock that night. The whole time, however, he had been brooding on what he had discovered. He decided to walk from London Bridge station, thinking that the exercise might clear his brain. It seemed to be beyond doubt that Lady Greville had had two pregnancies aborted. He tried to still the prejudices that conjured up. It didn't necessarily mean she was a loose woman. As youngsters they had giggled about the occasional young woman of their own acquaintance who had gone pink and rounded on a long holiday, and come back thin and chastened. Sir Walter clearly knew nothing about it. Perhaps it was only she who didn't want a child. Her husband could still have been its father. But what about the earlier one? He couldn't work it out precisely from what the nurse had said, but that seemed to have occurred after the death of her first husband, and before she remarried. Morton felt a pang of sympathy for her, recently widowed and finding herself pregnant. But surely if it had been her husband's child she would have wanted to keep it? She had married Sir Walter just a year after being widowed, and must have known him much longer. It was always possible that they had disregarded the conventions, and that the first child was his. Morton found this supposition violently disagreeable. He embarked on a brisk march to rid his mind of these unsavoury conjectures, until, finding himself in Moorgate, he was drawn towards Finsbury Circus.

It was still and peaceful in the lamp-light. He walked round to the north-east quadrant and looked towards number nine. Even allowing for the slightly earlier hour, it was difficult to see how Mrs Roberts could be so sure it was Applin she had seen. Morton crossed to the gardens in the centre, and seated himself on a bench. Had she been here, one could have accepted her assertions unreservedly, however dark the night. His eyes strayed upwards. There was a light on the second floor. He counted the windows. It was her boudoir. No doubt she was reading to pass the time, or to escape temporarily from the pressures on her. Morton felt an odd sense of shame at having pried out her secret.

As he pondered, he realized that he had been conscious of approaching footsteps, which had now stopped. He looked around him, but could see nothing. Then, looking again at the house, he saw someone at the front door. A man, bulky, in evening dress. He seemed to be fumbling at the lock. Morton started to his feet, then he saw the door was open and the man was withdrawing a key. Dumbfounded he watched as the door was closed quietly, then sat down again to await events. All was quiet for some ten minutes, then the light in Lady Greville's boudoir was extinguished. Almost immediately the central lamp in her bedroom was lit, and she crossed to the window to pull down the blind. For a moment her body was silhouetted against it, then a huge menacing shadow engulfed her, hands on her breasts. There was a ripple of excited laughter, and then the curtains were drawn.

Morton felt sick with disgust, angry at his own mawkish stupidity. He watched for a further twenty minutes; then the light in the bedroom was extinguished. Moments later the front door opened and the man emerged stealthily, his hat shading his face. But as he came down the steps into the light of the street-lamp, Morton could see that it was Hubert Winterslow.

CHAPTER _____

_____ SIXTEEN

'Well, that explains a lot,' remarked Bragg as they rattled down Fleet Street towards the West End. 'The Holborn Union, eh? I wonder how they do that one: sounds quite acrobatic!' He chuckled. 'What's the matter, lad? Are you feeling let down because one of your class has turned out to be human after all? I tell you, it's dangerous to put any woman on a pedestal. Damn it all, she was a widow at twenty-five with her best years before her. If you came from an ordinary background, it would be what you'd expect! One more thing we've discovered, though; she's got some go about her. She's not afraid of kicking over the traces. That will bear thinking on.'

They paid off the hansom, and entered the imposing hall of the club. Bragg asked for Applin, and the doorman directed them to the smoking room. They had sat there for some minutes when a club servant approached them.

'Are you waiting for Major Applin, sir?' he asked.

'Yes.'

'I'm sorry, but he's not in, and funnily enough his bed's not been slept in.'

'Christ Almighty! He's scarpered,' exclaimed Bragg. 'Get me the club secretary and be quick about it.' He paced around the room fuming, till an elderly gentleman came bristling up.

'Are you the secretary of this club?' demanded Bragg.

'I am indeed. May I know the reason for this unseemly conduct?'

'You may. Here is a warrant which empowers us to search the club premises, and in particular the rooms occupied by Major Applin.'

'Goodness gracious!' gasped the old man. 'Whatever has he done?'

'Nothing that need concern you,' replied Bragg brusquely. 'Now take us up to his rooms and see we're not disturbed. Have you got any deposit boxes in his name?'

'Not that I'm aware of. I will have it checked.'

They ascended three flights of stairs, and went along a narrow corridor. Then the secretary took out a pass-key and opened a door. 'These are Major Applin's rooms. I'm afraid they're not very grand, but not all of our members are wealthy . . .''

'Thank you,' said Bragg and closed the door on him. 'Quick, lad, you go through his bedroom. Look under the mattress and the furniture. See if there's anything that strikes you as odd. And don't forget the pockets of the clothes in the wardrobe. I'll start on the sitting room.'

There was little enough space in the bedroom, but Morton began methodically to search. He lifted all the furniture to see if anything was hidden underneath, turned back the carpet, stripped the bed, and examined the outside of the curtains. He took out all the clothes from the wardrobe and chest of drawers and examined them meticulously, but he could find nothing unexpected and nothing suspicious. He walked through to the sitting room.

'No luck,' he said.

'Have a look at this,' replied Bragg. 'It's a letter from our friend Plowright. Applin clearly told him about our enquiries and the probability that we'd exhume Greville. I'll give him "Keep me in touch with developments"! You know, these buggers have been swapping every bit of information they could get. We can't rely on anything they've said about each other. We could have a damned great conspiracy on our hands.'

'Anything I can do here?'

'Just go through the bookcase, will you, while I finish this desk.'

Applin's reading seemed to have been undemanding, to say the least. Morton noticed *The Moonstone, The Woman in White, East Lynne*, as well as Kipling and books on the regiments of the British Army. On the bottom shelf was a pile of *Strand Magazines*, their pages dog-eared to mark the instalments of the Sherlock Holmes stories.

'Applin seems to have a decided interest in crime,' he remarked.

'Does he now?' murmured Bragg. 'Come and have a look at this.'

He was staring at the sheet of paper. At the top had been drawn a rough rectangle; the top left-hand corner of which had been blocked off by another rectangle. Around this second rectangle the letters A B C and D were placed, seemingly haphazardly. The rest of the page was covered with lines of writing, in a script that consisted of curving undulating lines interspersed with dots.

'It looks as if it's in Arabic, or Hindustani,' said Morton. 'He did serve in India.'

'I've been staring at this for five minutes now,' replied Bragg, 'and the more I stare, the more I think it's a plan of the hall at the Grevilles' house, and this rectangle the stairs coming down. What the letters stand for, I don't know, but maybe the writing will tell us. Try and get it translated, lad, and quick. The British Museum would be your best bet. Now let's go and get a general alert out for Applin. And while we're about it we'll pull Plowright in as well.'

'I was just thinking, Joe,' mused the desk-sergeant, 'this description is practically the same as that of a man run over last night. Just a minute . . . Yes, his name was Applin. Found in Noble Street around one o'clock this morning. Detective Constable Thompson has it in hand.'

'Is he in?'

'No. I expect he's got his head down by now.'

'Is the body at the mortuary?'

'I expect so.'

When Bragg and Morton arrived in Noble Street, they could tell where the accident had happened by the knot of children gathered there.

'Go on. Clear off, you lot,' commanded Bragg. 'Go and play somewhere else.' The children withdrew reluctantly, but continued to watch from a nearby doorway.

On the pavement was a scattering of sand through which blood had seeped black and sticky. Morton flapped at the flies feeding on it, so that they rose in a cloud, to resettle immediately. There were three foot of scarring along the high kerbstone and a loose flake of stone where the iron-shod wheel had mounted the pavement. On the wall at this point was a scrape of dark green paint with wood splinters adhering to the brickwork. Below it were rags of skin and hair.

'Christ! That doesn't look like an accident to me,' said Bragg. 'You'd have had to force the horse practically on to the pavement to get the front wheel up that kerb. Here, you kids! Get some buckets of water and a brush, and clean up this mess, will you?'

They walked to Golden Lane mortuary in glum silence, Morton steeling himself for the revolting sight of a mangled body. As they entered, they bumped into Dr Burney.

'Applin?' he repeated with his loose smile. 'No he's not here yet. By great good fortune they brought him down to Bart's, though what they thought we could do, goodness only knows. However, I had a look at him myself. There was a large contusion in the middle of the back, probably caused by the shaft of the carriage or whatever it was. He seems to have been dragged along for a little way, and there's not much flesh remaining on the left side of his head. There are clear marks of two separate wheels passing over his rib cage . . . completely crushed, must have died instantly.'

'The kerb there is six inches high,' said Bragg. 'Even if the pavement is only two and a half feet wide, it was a chance in a million that a runaway horse could drag its vehicle on to that pavement just when Major Applin was there.'

'These things do happen,' smiled Burney.

'I gave up believing in coincidence when little Sally Parkin left me for a boy with a bigger conker,' growled Bragg.

'Well, I wouldn't disagree with you, sergeant. Belonging to the Tory Party is beginning to be a chancy business around here. Indeed, I'm seriously considering joining the Liberals.'

• • •

Bragg and Morton spent the next day separately visiting livery stables and haulage firms, to see if any of their vehicles had been damaged over the weekend. They met again on the Wednesday morning in gloomy mood.

'What a bloody day,' complained Bragg. 'Do you know? I asked that sod Cotton for a couple of men to help us, told him it was a murder case now, and what did he say? "I haven't the resources to squander on detached-duty operations. You'd better go to the Commissioner." '

'Perhaps his wife's heard about our serenade.'

'Perhaps.' A momentary smile crossed Bragg's face. 'Ah well, anger just clouds your brain.'

'I suppose Applin's death means he wasn't the murderer,' suggested Morton.

'Unless we believe in the conspiracy theory, and assume Applin was the weak link that was knocked off before we broke him. In that case all we need to do is wait till there's only one left, and pick him up!'

'That wouldn't exactly cover us in glory.'

'No, it seems to me that your notion of the amateur detective is nearer the mark. You remember his daft request to be at the exhumation? And his excitement on Friday could have been because he thought he knew who'd done it. If so, the poor devil paid for his whistle with a vengeance.'

The desk-sergeant poked his head round the door. 'There's a bit in the *City Press* this morning about your man Applin; thought you might want to see it. Page five.'

Bragg spread the paper on his desk, and Morton went round to peer over his shoulder.

'Good God!'' exclaimed Bragg. 'It's about the missing head. That'll sell a few papers this morning.'

'Applin speaking from the grave,' remarked Morton.

'Miss Marsden must have seen him straight after our last interview.'

'Perhaps he was keeping her in touch with developments too . . . I don't like this, lad. If Applin was murdered for what he knew, then that lass is in danger too. Anybody reading this will be certain he told her everything. Blast it, she ought to be locked up for her own good.'

'I'm going down to the British Museum now. I'll call in at the office, and see her, or the editor. The least we can do is warn them.'

'Do anything you think best. We can't afford to find her body on a muck-heap.'

Catherine Marsden put down her pen with a smile of satisfaction. The royal family tree looked crisp and clear, yes, and elegant. It would go well across a treble column. She began to feel that smugness was her besetting sin. The circulation manager had just been up to tell her that the demand for that day's paper was so great, they were printing an extra run. And all because of her column! She hugged herself with delight. Not that it was completely her own work. The editor had altered it around quite a bit, but the basic draft had been hers. Indeed it had been mangled considerably less than the one about the inquest. Come to think of it Mr Tranter had been almost complimentary. After today's sales he'd be sure to admit they were on the right track . . . Success would be in her grasp.

There was a tap at the door, and a tall young man entered.

'Hello,' he said. 'I'm Constable Morton. We met the other day in Pall Mall.'

'Ah yes.' Catherine didn't know whether to stand up, or remain seated and hold out her hand. She compromised by waving him to a chair.

'Not that you could say we met properly. My name's James, and you, I gather, are Catherine Marsden.' He was very handsome with his close curly hair and wide smile. She put up a hand to smooth her hair, then checked herself in irritation.

'I must say you're looking very pleased with yourself this morning,' he went on in a bantering tone. 'It must be your birthday.'

'No. It's just that life is very satisfying at the moment.'

'What's that you're doing?'

'I've been asked to write a series about the royal family and its connection with the City. Nowadays it's fairly nebulous, and confined to ceremonial occasions, but in mediaeval times the country was governed from here. One could go back into Saxon times, but there's not a lot of source material, and I'm rather poor at mediaeval church Latin. So I'm starting with William the Conqueror.'

'Do you enjoy being a journalist?' he asked.

'Oh yes. I have a weakness for telling people what they ought to be thinking! In a way, I suppose it's not very different from being a policeman. We're both concerned about people.'

'As it happens, I'm here because I'm concerned about you.'

Catherine was momentarily taken aback. She had never been the recipient of quite such a direct flirtation, and on such a tenuous acquaintance, too. And yet although the tone was light, there was a seriousness behind it.

'I'm sure I can't think why,' she replied, and mentally kicked herself for sounding like a coquette.

'You have a piece in this morning's edition about Sir Walter Greville,' he said, the smile gone from his face.

'It's a matter of public interest,' she retorted defensively.

'It's perfectly proper, and there's nothing in it that isn't factual.'

'I'm sure that's true.' He was looking at her coolly, appraisingly, but there was nothing sexual in his glance. Catherine began to feel like a butterfly with a pin through her middle.

'You were really reporting a conversation with Major Applin, weren't you? When did you see him?'

'On Saturday morning. He came here and told me about a meeting he'd had with Sergeant Bragg the day before.'

'Did he give you any information you didn't publish?'

'Well, he wasn't very complimentary about the police. He said he would get there before they did. I disregarded that as being typical male exhibitionism.'

'Did you now?' he said with a grin. 'Did he say anything about what he was going to do, or where he was going to go?'

'Of course not,' Catherine replied with some asperity. 'Why ask me all these questions? You know that journalists have to protect their sources. If you want to know, ask him.'

'I'm afraid,' said the young man gravely, 'this is a source that you signally failed to protect. Major Applin is dead.'

'Dead? But he looked so well . . . oh! . . . Don't tell me he's been killed.'

'He was murdered on Sunday night; run over by some kind of vehicle in Noble Street. We haven't found it yet.'

'But if he was run over . . .'

'It wasn't an accident,' said the constable firmly. 'He was on a pavement two-foot-six wide, with a six-inch kerb. And for my money, he was running to get away.'

'But it's horrifying!' Catherine stared at him, unbelieving.

'We think that he was murdered for what he knew. And

the reason it happened on Sunday was that his murderer had read your article in Saturday's *City Press*.'

Catherine flinched. 'I had no idea . . .'

'I'm not saying you're responsible for his death. He was killed because he was trying to be clever. What concerns us now is that the murderer may feel Applin told you everything he knew. That's why I want you to take special precautions.'

Catherine tried to control her distress. 'What is it you want me to do?'

'Where do you live?'

'Nine-five Park Lane, with my parents.'

'Very well. I'll be back around half past four, and I'll escort you home. I'll call for you tomorrow morning at eight to bring you into the City. For the next few days don't take any cabs unless you are accompanied; use the omnibus instead. If you walk anywhere take the main roads, and try to keep amongst other people where you can. Don't go to any of the seedy areas of London, it would be asking for trouble; and don't be out after dark.'

'Goodness! What a catalogue.'

'It's important, until we have caught the murderer. With any luck we'll have him in a few days.'

'Very well, I'll do as you wish.'

'Good,' he smiled reassuringly. 'I'll have a word with your editor so that he's aware of what's happening, and then I must be off to the British Museum . . . I don't suppose you've got any research to do there this morning,' he added lightly.

'No, I'm afraid not.'

'I wouldn't have you think that I spend my time there, or I might feature in one of your articles next week, headed "Policeman studies oriental languages at ratepayers' expense".' He drew a folded paper from his pocket. 'We found this in Major Applin's desk. We think it's some notes he's written in an eastern language. He did spend some time in India.'

Catherine pulled the paper towards her, and studied it. 'I think I can save you a journey,' she said in amusement. 'It's not Arabic, or anything like that, it's Gregg's shorthand. I began to study it at first, then switched to Pitman's, but I remember enough to recognize it.'

'Can you read it?' asked Morton in excitement.

'You are asking a great deal,' she protested. 'People can't read their own shorthand after a week . . . Let me see.' She examined it carefully. 'Well, I can't read much of it, but this squiggle is certainly "stairs", and I think that's "eleven". You could probably get someone to decipher the whole of it at the Gregg school in High Holborn.'

'You're marvellous! Any time you feel like giving up journalism, come and join us.'

'The police don't know women exist.'

'Ouch! See you at half past four.'

'Shorthand?' asked Bragg. 'Well I'm damned. What does it say?'

'I don't know. I went down to High Holborn, but the school was closed for the holidays. I've sent a message to the principal, so we'll just have to wait.'

'Is there no one else can read it?'

'It won't be easy to find anyone. The Gregg system is likely only a few years old. Most shorthand writers use Pitman's. Even Catherine switched to Pitman's from Gregg's.'

' "Even Catherine" eh? My God, lad, your affections are like a hot-air balloon. One minute you're scraping the rooftops, then a little warmth and you're soaring into the clouds. But be careful, it can be cold and miserable up there.'

'Our relationship is totally platonic,' replied Morton with a grin. 'I'm merely protecting her.'

'She'd be better protected if we could catch the murderer. I've spent all the morning going round in circles. It could be any one of four people. Hayward I see as an outsider, but he was in fact out on bail last Saturday. We can't arrest all of them, we'd look idiots . . . And yet we're so near. Blast it! I can't think straight without being able to chew my moustache.'

When Catherine received Lady Greville's note, she determined to carry out Morton's instructions to the letter. She ignored a cab that was standing near the office, and decided to go on foot via Gresham Street and Moorgate, which were sure to be crowded. She kept well in to the fronts of the buildings, and scrutinized every man as he approached. Receiving some distinctly prurient looks in return, she realized the absurdity of her conduct. No doubt the constable was trying to help, but she wasn't totally without resource. Perhaps he had exaggerated the danger so that she would agree to his escorting her home. He had certainly been rather forward, though at the time she had considered he was merely trying to lessen the impact of his words. She smiled at the thought of her father's reaction to a London bobby calling on her. Mummy would take it in her stride, of course, but Daddy would be outraged. He was really a rather superior kind of constable, however; he spoke well, and his manner at times had suggested someone well-versed in social dalliance. In some says she would have preferred to keep him away from her home. He hadn't reacted one way or another, when she'd said she lived in Park Lane. He probably had no idea what it was like. But if he actually saw her parents' house he would be sure to be put off. Not that it was a great mansion, but it was undeniably the home of someone wealthy. Perhaps she could get him to leave her by the mews cottage, and she could get into the house through the garden. She was just murmuring 'James Morton', to herself when she realized she had arrived at West Street, and must gather her thoughts for the interview. It would not be easy. After the events of the last fortnight Lady Greville must be overwrought. It would be better to let the interview develop, rather than try to control it by her questions. She straightened her jabot, settled her hat on her head, and pulled the bell. After a few moments she heard footsteps within, and the door was opened by Lady Greville herself.

'You must be Catherine Marsden,' she said with a smile. 'Come in. I'm afraid I have only two servants at the moment, and they are both at liberty in the afternoons.'

Catherine followed Lady Greville up the grand staircase, along the corridor, past the open door of the large drawing room, and up to the next floor.

'What a magnificent house,' she said in an effort to start a conversation.

'It's been in the Greville family for two generations, but the lease is being surrendered at the end of the month. Let's go into my late husband's study.'

Catherine glanced round the room with interest, then settling herself on a chair in front of the desk, took out her notebook.

'It's very good of you to spare me a few minutes, in the present circumstances, Lady Greville,' she said.

'In our society, a widow seldom has anything pressing to do. I ought to be grateful to you; it will help to pass the afternoon.' Lady Greville's voice was cool and controlled, but with a timbre that Catherine could not identify. She turned from the window and gazed at Catherine for a moment. 'So you are a correspondent for the *City Press*?' she asked. 'How were you able to obtain such a position?'

'My father introduced me to the editor, and I was offered a probationary post to write a column which would interest women readers.'

'Do you think it will be made permanent?'

'I hope so. I suppose it will depend on whether enough women like what I write . . . and take the trouble to let the editor know.'

Lady Greville gave her a twisted smile. 'I don't know why I am giving you an interview. I am not at all pleased with your paper at the moment. It has printed the most scandalous rumours about my late husband, and there was a quite scurrilous paragraph about the coroner last week.'

Catherine almost sprang to her own defence, then realized that Lady Greville would not know she had written them. Certainly the present interview would be terminated quickly if she discovered it.

'In the last month, the *City Press* has descended to the level of a political lampoon,' went on Lady Greville. 'Tilting at institutional windmills, smearing public figures . . .'

'Are you suggesting they have a political objective?' asked Catherine.

'My husband was a Tory MP, and the City is solidly Tory. Only the Liberals could profit from the kind of campaign your newspaper is waging.'

'But there must be some truth in it,' ventured Catherine. 'Otherwise it would never be printed.'

'That kind of journalist can concoct a report out of one per cent fact, and the rest speculation,' replied Lady Greville contemptuously.

Catherine had an uncomfortable feeling that she was

being baited and decided to switch the subject. 'You must be one of the most interesting and successful women of your generation, Lady Greville. I am sure many of our readers would like to emulate you, if they knew how. Have you any advice to give them?' Even as she spoke, the words sounded trite and silly. Nevertheless, Lady Greville considered them seriously.

'Ultimately, it's a matter of temperament,' she replied briskly. 'Most women can't organize their lives enough to succeed. Once their mothers have arranged their marriage they relax into feckless torpor until the time comes to marry off their own daughters.'

Catherine smiled at the thought of her own mother's indolence. 'But surely one's background counts for something?' she asked.

'Of course. But one can rise above one's background. One can never overcome ingrained sloth. I was the daughter of a small country landowner, who spent his time running after the local gentlewomen, while I ran his house. When I was twenty I manoeuvred him into arranging a marriage for me with a widower of fifty. He was very wealthy, and a considerable figure in the county. In that way I was brought into an entirely different social stratum . . . And the same happened again when I married Sir Walter.'

'You feel that women should be more alive to the opportunities that offer themselves?' asked Catherine.

'I'm saying that women should create opportunities for themselves.' Lady Greville glanced at the ornate clock on the mantelpiece.

'If all you want is marriage and security,' she went on, 'then the present social system will provide it. If you want something more interesting, more satisfying, you have to be prepared to forswear Lotus-land and fight!'

Again Catherine heard a hard edge of excitement in Lady Greville's voice.

'But most people would regard you as exemplifying the domestic and social virtues of our present system.'

'Then most people would be wrong. That's another thing that women will have to learn—how to use men in the way women have been used by them for centuries.'

'Are you saying that you used Sir Walter in this way?' asked Catherine in a neutral tone.

'We both used each other. I built him up into what passes for a politician in the City . . . though goodness knows he was never much more than lobby-fodder. In return I acquired a thorough knowledge of the political world and the people in it.'

Catherine was taken aback at the detachment of this comment. 'And what does the future hold for you now he is dead?' she asked.

'Now I am free to begin the fight for women's place in society.'

'But surely that has been going on for a generation?' Catherine objected.

'Yes, it has, in a wishy-washy woman's way. Nothing has really happened since the repeal of the Contagious Diseases Acts. That created a real militancy in us. But now that decent women are no longer exposed to being arbitrarily declared as common prostitutes, they've relapsed into accepting their freedom in their menfolk's good time. What we must do is to regenerate militancy in women, to compel men to treat us as equals. It's no good trying to infiltrate business and the professions. When do you think women will be able to have a career equal to men in law, medicine, or the Church? No, we have to fight for the franchise, because it's only through the ballot-box that we will be able to obtain our rights.'

'How will you set about it?' asked Catherine sardonically. 'A strike in the bed-chamber?' The attempted witticism fell leaden and dull.

'We shall have to be prepared to forsake the decorous, elegant image men have cast us in. We must disrupt public life, hold men up to ridicule, even make the country ungovernable . . . You look surprised. It can be done! Fifty per cent of the population are women . . . and yet they have accepted a position of degradation and dependence that has no moral or practical justification. I tell you, we can do it!'

After this peroration, an uneasy silence fell. Catherine saw Lady Greville glance again at the clock and frown, but she made no attempt to bring the interview to an end. Catherine looked at her shorthand. Her pencil had become blunt, and she doubted if she would be able to read some of her outlines. Next time she must remember to bring more than one pencil. She cast around in her mind for another topic to explore.

'You seem to have rather unorthodox views on marriage, Lady Greville.'

'If you mean that I don't believe in love as the basis for marriage, you are right. But then no one does. Part of the trouble is that women try to invest what is a purely commercial transaction with an aura of romance. To my mind, a marriage should be useful to both parties; it should allow both of them to achieve their aspirations. Once it falls below this ideal it should cease. I have already mentioned my first marriage. It gave me what I then required for my ultimate purpose; and if my husband was not very capable between the sheets, I had brought Tom Barnes, my groom, as part of my dowry . . . You look shocked! That's because, for all your liberated appearance, you are still a stereotype.' Lady Greville laughed harshly.

'Tom Barnes and I grew up together, we ran wild over my father's estate, and with all that coition going on around us, it was natural we should try our hand at it . . . And, of course, he was useful to me when John had outlived his usefulness . . . He was killed accidentally, when we were out riding. Being a man, he couldn't bear to be a less accomplished rider than I. That's what I mean by women creating opportunities for themselves . . . I knew, of course, that John would try to follow me over the wall. Perhaps his horse had more sense than he had, or else it knew of the drop on the other side. But it wasn't my fault it refused, and threw him at the wall, was it? When I rode round through the gate, I found Tom Barnes bending over him . . . but he was dead.'

Catherine's mind was a turmoil of outraged comprehension and fear. She should pretend she didn't understand . . . bring the interview to an end and get away. But it mustn't be obvious . . . Her numbed brain tried to formulate an excuse. She looked up and saw that Lady Greville was regarding her in malevolent triumph. Then she cocked her head. 'Ah, I think I heard the bell,' she said. 'Excuse me a moment.' She crossed to the door, closing it behind her, and Catherine heard the key turn in the lock.

Morton went up to Catherine's room on the stroke of half past four. He was disappointed that she was not there, but her desk was strewn with books and papers, so she was not far away. He went over to see what she was working on. Still the City and royalty, by the look of it. On her blotter was a new family tree, headed 'Plantagenets', with the kings underlined in red. Henry II, Richard I, John, Henry III, Edward I, Edward II, Edward III, Richard II. There was something odd about it, thought Morton, though he didn't know why. He wished he'd read history instead of languages, it would have been much more use at this particular moment.

'Are you waiting for Miss Marsden?' A coatless youth was standing in the doorway.

'Yes.'

'She went up to interview Lady Greville an hour ago. She shouldn't be long.'

'Thanks.'

He looked at the family tree again in irritation. What was it that was gnawing away in his mind? Why should Catherine want to interview Lady Greville? . . . Greville! Then he was running, crashing down the stairs, feet pounding on the pavements, hurling himself across streets under the noses of horses, lungs bursting. He clattered up the stairs to Bragg's room and stood leaning on the desk, his shoulders heaving.

'There were . . . eight Plantagenet kings,' he gasped. 'Catherine's there now.' And he was gone.

Catherine rattled vainly at the door, but it was firmly locked. The window overlooked the garden, and there was no possibility of attracting attention. She raised the lower sash and peered out. There was no one in the gardens to hear her cries. Below her was a paved basement area. If she tried to escape that way she would fall to her death. She felt the curtains; they would hold her weight, but were so strong she could never tear them into strips. In any case she could not make a rope from them that would reach to the ground.

Then the door was thrown open and Lady Greville re-entered followed by a burly middle-aged man. She glanced round the room, taking in the open window and Catherine crouched in her chair.

'At least you have the wit to realize your position,' she remarked, closing and locking the window. 'This is the girl, Hubert.'

'But why is she a danger to us?'

'You've seen the paper. Applin must have told her all he knew.'

'We can't be certain of that,' protested Winterslow.

'Do we have to be certain?' she asked scornfully. 'It's enough that he might have done. Anyway, she's guessed.'

Winterslow looked doubtfully at Catherine's tear-streaked face.

'We can't just kill her . . .' he muttered.

'Why not? Why is she any different from Walter? You are a miserable milksop, Hubert. Shall I have to call Tom to finish her off too?'

'But we can't do it here. The newspaper people know she came to see you.'

'Yes we can. Tom's filling the bath with water. All you have to do is drown her here, then he can take her body tonight and throw it in the river. When they do the post-mortem examination they'll find she drowned, that's all.'

'They'll never believe it. Why should she do away with herself?'

'Girls do it all the time, an indiscreet love affair, a disgrace to her family . . . Yes, that's it,' she smiled sadistically. 'You'd better deflower her first, you'll enjoy that.'

'No!' cried Winterslow loudly. 'I won't do it.'

Lady Greville gave him a hard calculating look, then opened the door. 'Tom!' she cried.

The man who answered her call was of medium height, rough-looking, and wiry. He had about him, thought Catherine, the cocky assertiveness of one who delighted in his physical strength. At the sight of him Catherine felt panic rise in her throat.

'Take the girl and drown her,' ordered Lady Greville calmly.

Tom grinned and took a step towards Catherine, brushing Winterslow aside. Then as he made to seize her, Winterslow grabbed him by the collar and threw him staggering back till he fell with a clatter in the fireplace. With the speed of a snake, Tom was on his feet again, an iron poker in his hand. Winterslow put out his hands to grapple with him, but Tom brought the poker crashing down on his forehead. As Winterslow tottered Tom tripped him and in savage frenzy struck at his head till he was still. Catherine was overwhelmed by waves of nausea. She dimly saw Tom wiping his poker on Winterslow's jacket, then look up in her direction.

'I suppose it was inevitable.' Lady Greville's voice held only a cold detachment. 'He was a stupid man . . . Now the girl, and be careful not to hurt her.'

Catherine stumbled out of the chair and seized hold of the curtains. Tom laughed, and grabbing her by the middle jerked her free. She felt herself swung into the air, across his shoulder, and began to kick at him and pummel his back with her fists. She managed to get hold of the door jamb and hung on desperately; but he took a few paces back into the room, then burst through the doorway and into the passage. He now held her feet imprisoned with his arm. She grabbed at the pictures on the wall but they eluded her. She could sense that he was preparing to turn through the bathroom door, and spread her arms wide to catch at the jamb. For a moment she held on, then he gave a fierce lunge, and broke her grip. For the first time she gave a screech of fear and despair, then she was pulled down off his shoulder. The shock of the cold water on her feet revived her panic, and she began scratching and beating at his face. Now she was being forced down, she could feel the water around her shoulders. She pushed hard with her feet on the bottom of the bath, holding desperately on to its sides with both hands. Then she felt the pressure slacken, heard Lady Greville's voice remote and urgent.

'I thought I heard a noise.'

Then Tom suddenly thrust down on her shoulders, the back of her head hit the bath and she lost consciousness.

Morton threw himself at the front door, but it was locked. Wasting no more time, he climbed on to the area railings and from there got a precarious foothold on the windowsill. Holding on to the upper sash he kicked at the lower window, feeling a sharp sting as the slivers of glass sliced into his flesh. Then he crouched on the sill and pushed at the leaded window within. It gave under the pressure of his hand, but obstinately refused to be dislodged. Morton curled himself up until he could get his head and shoulders against it, then, using the outer window frame as a lever, pushed with all his strength. There was a squealing noise as a metal bar buckled under the strain, and suddenly he was catapulted on to the floor of the hall. He picked himself up and threw open the door to see Bragg purple and panting just beginning to mount the steps. He turned and raced up the staircase, looking briefly in the drawing room, then on to the next floor. He peered cautiously into Lady Greville's boudoir, but it was empty, with nothing out of place. Her bedroom likewise. He glanced perfunctorily into her dressing room, and as he did so sensed that someone was behind him. He twisted to one side, and felt a searing pain down his right arm. He turned and grappled with the man, pushing him against the wall and bringing up his knee hard into his crotch. They fell together, writhing and twisting to the floor.

'Hold on, lad,' he heard Bragg's gasp. 'I'll have the darbies on him if you'll only keep still. If I had a neddy I'd put the bastard to sleep.'

'It must be the bathroom opposite,' cried Morton.

Bragg tried the door, but it was locked. He took two steps back and flung himself at it. There was a splintering of wood and the door swung back. By the window, erect and disdainful, stood Lady Greville, in the bath the limp body of Catherine Marsden.

'Get the cuffs on her, while I fish this one out. Put her in the broom cupboard with Charlie boy, then come and give me a hand.'

When Morton had got the pair safely locked up he returned to find Bragg wrenching at the girl's corset. 'I think she's alive,' he cried. 'Here, grab one of her legs. That's it, now slide her off the bed and hold her upside down.'

Holding a leg each they suspended her with her head touching the carpet, while Bragg gently slapped her back.

'What bloody silly clothes women wear,' he grumbled. 'They're so tight-laced they can't breathe properly, and now her petticoats have fallen over her face we can't tell whether she's draining out or not. Have a look and see, lad. I can hold her for a minute.'

Morton dropped on his knee and raised the sodden dress. There was so much water on the floor he couldn't tell whether any had come from her mouth. He glanced at her bared breasts; they moved slightly with her breathing. Then looking down again, he saw that her eyes had opened.

He backed away guiltily. 'She's conscious,' he cried.

'Good, help me get her back on the bed, and find some blankets. And then telephone to the police station and a doctor. I think there's an instrument in the study.'

Bragg wrapped the girl in the blankets, murmuring reassuringly to her, but she just stared fixedly before her, saying nothing.

'Sergeant, sergeant!' came Morton's voice down the corridor.

'What is it lad? I'm busy.'

'There's a man's body here with its head battered in; still warm.' Morton appeared in the doorway. 'Guess who it is.'

'Winterslow?'

'Right first time.'

Bragg looked at the swathed form of the girl on the bed. 'Poor little lass,' he said. 'I reckon she's been through it. And you, lad, you'd better get yourself to the hospital, you're like a walking slaughter-house.'

CHAPTER ———— ———— SEVENTEEN

'I can't say it's worked out the way I wanted it,' said Sir William plaintively. 'You'll know the coroner has resigned. I gather the Home Office is pushing some Professor of Law on us, a QC.'

'I hadn't heard, sir.'

'Still, we've done our best, Bragg, we've done our best. Can't understand a woman like that. Fancy doing . . . it with a groom.'

'She seemed to be a lady of exceptional tastes, sir.'

'If you ask me, they are both animals.'

'She deceived everybody she came into contact with, nevertheless,' remarked Bragg. 'Poor old Applin went along like a lamb into a lion's den to tell her he thought she'd killed her husband. I've had his notes deciphered since I wrote my report. As we suspected, he did go back to Finsbury Square that night. Apparently he intended to persuade Sir Walter that he couldn't maintain his position for long on the basis of bribes and threats. When he arrived there, the door was ajar, and he could see Sir Walter's body in the middle of the floor, with Lady Greville and two men standing around it. Why he withdrew I don't know. Perhaps he suspected foul play. Anyway he clearly realized that the evidence given at the inquest didn't square with what he'd seen.'

'Which was why he sent the card to the coroner.'

'He seems to have been a curious kind of man. I think it made him feel superior, watching us blundering about, when his secret knowledge could have solved it for us.'

'He certainly paid dearly for it,' said Sir William. 'He clearly didn't expect her to counter-attack so quickly or so decisively.'

'It's an interesting speculation that at the very moment when Tom Barnes was running down Major Applin, she was in the arms of Winterslow. I reckon the knowledge would have increased her pleasure.'

'Yes, well . . .' The Commissioner cleared his throat. 'I suppose the girl will be well enough to give evidence?' he asked gloomily.

'No doubt of it, sir. They're very resilient at that age. And the groom has made a full confession. It was he who went to Fulford and hacked off Greville's head. They'd been warned by Winterslow, who'd received a letter from Applin saying there was to be an exhumation. Barnes buried the head in some woods. He can't remember where. He seems to have been her confidant as well as her stallion. According to him, Lady Greville held out to Winterslow that she would marry him if he would get rid of Sir Walter for her.'

'But your report says that Barnes killed him.'

'True enough. Winterslow went back to the house briefly that night. Sir Walter came down to let him out of the house again, and Winterslow pushed him down the stairs. But as you'd expect, the fall only stunned him, and Winterslow hadn't the stomach to finish him off. However, Lady Greville had warned the groom to be around, and he bludgeoned Greville to death with one of the bronze statues.'

'Have we run it to earth yet?'

'No. I doubt if we will. Barnes says he threw it into the river from London Bridge . . . It was only Morton's realization that the statuette of a woman had been substituted that got us there in time.'

'So Barnes has killed three people in all: Sir Walter, Major Applin, and Winterslow.'

'We can add Lady Greville's first husband to the list. It seems Barnes found him still alive, and finished him off with a brick.'

'Has he confessed to that?' asked the Commissioner in surprise.

'Volunteered it, more like. He's boasting about them.'

'And did Lady Greville know about that?'

'If she didn't, it was because she chose not to.'

'I find it difficult to believe a woman like that could exist,' remarked Sir William with a shudder. 'I suppose if they'd got away with Sir Walter's murder, then Winterslow's wife would have been the next.'

'Perhaps . . . Though I don't think Lady Greville would ever have kept her promise. What she wanted was her freedom.'

'But it wasn't just that, was it? I mean, apart from being unsuccessful politically, Sir Walter had been stealing her money.'

'That's true,' said Bragg thoughtfully. 'I suppose a woman of her kidney wouldn't forgive him that . . . And once he'd let on he knew about the abortions, he was as good as dead.'

'Presumably she could tell they weren't by her husband?' said the Commissioner self-consciously. 'I don't know much about these things.'

'I reckon she wasn't going to be lumbered with them, whoever was the father,' replied Bragg. 'I think she saw herself at the first woman Member of Parliament.'

Sir William's gloom returned. 'You know, the politicians aren't going to like this, Bragg, particularly the Tories.'

'And yet it was the Prime Minister who gave us the vital clue.'

'Really, Bragg?' The Commissioner's face brightened.

'Oh yes, sir. If Lord Salisbury hadn't mentioned Sir Walter's feminist speeches, and joked about Lady Greville writing them, we'd never have begun to suspect her.'

'That's true, Bragg. You're right . . .' Sir William smiled. 'Yes . . . I'm sure the Prime Minister would be interested to know that.'